LONG TIME GONE

A ROUGH RIDERS NOVELLA

LORELEI JAMES

Long Time Gone

Rough Riders Novella 16.5

Copyright © 2015 LJLA, LLC

Cover design by: Meredith Blair –
www.authorsangels.com

ISBN: 978-1-941869-00-0

Other titles from Lorelei James

Rough Riders Series
(in reading order)

Authors note: *This story runs simultaneously with the Carson McKay and Carolyn West storyline in Cowboy Take Me Away— two days prior to Carson and Carolyn's wedding...*

Chapter One

Calvin McKay wasn't a fan of weddings.

But since his twin brother Carson was getting hitched in two days, he had to slap on a smile and deal with all the crap that went along with it.

At least there wasn't a bachelor party. It wasn't Carolyn, his brother's bride-to-be, who'd put the kibosh on that, but the groom himself. Carson claimed everything leading up to his nuptials had been one long-ass bachelor party, and Cal didn't disagree.

From what he could tell, the ceremony would be a small, simple affair. Nothing like Cal's buddy Joey's wedding. Such pomp and circumstance. He'd expect something like that for the president, the queen, or the pope—not for a sheep rancher from Hulett marrying a hairdresser from Cheyenne. But the bride's daddy owned the largest western clothing store in Wyoming and he'd spared no expense for the wedding.

But by the day's end, Cal had pitied Joey. His wife's family was a bunch of assholes. So he couldn't help but wonder... Had Joey overlooked that because he loved her?

Cal had already been asked to overlook the shitty things Carolyn's family had done to his brother. That hadn't sat well with him, but he'd agreed not to make waves. So he'd rather be anywhere else than headed to meet another member of the West family.

Although if this sister looked anything like the beautiful Carolyn, it wouldn't be a chore to stand across from her on the altar on Sunday afternoon. It'd be a bonus if she had those same great tits. Cal shot his brother a look and bit back a smirk. He'd have two black eyes if Carson had a clue what he'd just been thinking.

"I need some alone time with Caro to talk about some stuff," Carson said. "So you can entertain the kid sister for us, right?"

Kid sister. Great. "Sure."

By the time they pulled up, Carolyn was already waiting for them outside the ice cream shop. Alone. Maybe her sister had decided not to come.

Cal knew he couldn't be so lucky. He had a strange feeling about this.

Carson bailed out of the truck so fast he'd left the keys in the ignition and the driver's door open. Cal opted not to watch his brother stake his claim on his fiancée, right there in the damn parking lot. After he shut his brother's door, he ambled to the front entrance and waited for them to end their reunion.

The happy couple finally unclenched their mouths and strolled toward him, arms still wrapped around each other. Seeing Carson acting so possessive with Carolyn just meant it was ten times more fun to watch him blow his top when he thought someone was horning in on his territory—even his own brother.

Carolyn said, "Hey, Cal."

"Hey, Carolyn, You're lookin' good today." He pushed off the wall and moved in closer as if he planned to hug her. He swore he heard Carson growl. "You sure you wanna marry this guy?" He jerked his thumb toward his twin. "He's kinda bossy. I'm much more laid back."

"I'm gonna lay you out flat if you keep tryin' to steal my woman, jackass," Carson snarled.

He shrugged, then offered Carson a conniving smile. "She's fair game until you say them vows, so I just want her to be sure."

The way Carolyn looked at Carson, her face shining with adoration, and said, "I'm sure," gave Cal a little pang of envy.

"Your loss."

Carson muttered something about Cal losing his teeth as he led the way into the Ice Cream Palace.

The first person Cal saw was *her*.

One look at the tiny blonde standing in the middle of the room and he knew he was in trouble.

Big trouble.

Life-altering trouble.

He'd never thought that bolt of lightning shit would ever happen to him, but it had. He wondered if anyone else smelled ozone.

"Sweet mother of god, I think I'm in love."

"Oh, for Christsake," Carson muttered beside him.

"*Please* tell me that's your sister," Cal said to Carolyn.

Cal's focus remained so intently on the hot little number not-so-innocently licking an ice cream cone that Carolyn had to snap her fingers in front of his eyes to get his attention. "Hey, McKay, focus."

"What?"

"Yes, that's my younger sister. She's sixteen. Do you hear me? *Six. Teen.*"

Cal managed to tear his gaze away from the curvaceous blonde, giving Carolyn an ornery grin. "Well, darlin', she ain't always gonna be sixteen."

The blonde sauntered over, those big blue eyes focused entirely on him.

Sweet heaven, she packed a powerful punch.

She said, "Please tell me you're not my future brother-in-law?"

"I'm not. But darlin' girl, I'm damn near certain I'm your future husband."

She peered at him from beneath lowered lashes. "Then maybe you and me better get acquainted...?"

"Calvin McKay. You can call me Cal. Better yet, call me anytime you want."

"Jesus, Cal," Carson complained. "Give it a rest."

After Carolyn elbowed Carson in the ribs, he offered the woman his hand. "Kimi? Glad to meet you. Caro has told me a lot about you."

Kimi. The name suited her. Short and cute.

"Likewise." Kimi's gaze left Cal's and her eyes narrowed on Carson. "Make my sister happy or I'll gut you like a trout."

"Kimi!" Carolyn exclaimed.

But Kimi ignored her sister, and focused on Cal again with such intensity his dick got hard. "Let's leave the lovebirds alone and you can tell me why such a handsome man as yourself is still single."

"Because I was waitin' for you." Cal slipped his arm around Kimi's shoulder. As he steered her toward the back booth, he said, "Your ice cream is melting, sweetheart. You'd better eat up."

"Would you like a taste?" she said.

"Of you? Absolutely. I don't give a damn about the ice cream."

Kimi laughed. "You are bad."

"Nope. I'm just testing the waters to see if you are."

When Cal tried to scoot next to her in the booth, she shoved him back out. "Not so fast, partner. Sit on your own side." She raised an eyebrow. "And put your hands on the table where I can see them."

Cal grinned. So the little flirt wasn't a pushover. "So let's start with the basics."

"Okay. Like what?"

Like I want you to tell me everything about you.

Maybe he'd better take a broader approach. "I don't know much about your family. I sure had no idea that Carolyn had such a luscious—I mean lovely—little sister."

She rolled her eyes and kept nibbling on her cone.

"I do know there's some long-standing feud between the Wests and the McKays. When your brother Harland found out about Carolyn datin' Carson, he beat the shit out of him."

"Classy of him, doncha think? Who else gets a welcome to the family like that?" she said with complete sarcasm. "Carolyn said my other brothers were just as bad with threats and crap."

"All of them were except for Thomas. He was decent."

Kimi looked over her shoulder and then back at him. "Between us? I think Thomas will end up giving Carolyn away since my dad ain't gonna show for the wedding."

"You think your sister knows that?"

"Yeah. I just don't know why it matters to her if he does or doesn't show. It's not like they've ever been close."

"Why not?"

"Because our mom sent Carolyn away to Catholic school when she was still a girl. Then I pitched such a fit about missing my sister that I got sent away a year later. We only come home for the holidays and half the summer." She frowned. "Except this year, after Carolyn graduated, my dad said there was no need for me to come home at all. This was after my parents couldn't be bothered to come up to Billings for Carolyn's high school graduation. I hated how disappointed Carolyn was. I know she'll be facing that disappointment on Sunday and once again there's not a damn thing I can do about it."

Cal didn't know what to say to that. Carson had given him the bare bones story about the West girls being sent off to school, but he'd never understood why. "I doubt our dad will show either. But Carson couldn't give a damn."

Kimi smirked. "That's where Carson and I are alike. Speaking of alike...you and Carson are twins."

"Yep."

"I wasn't kidding about coming after him with a knife if he hurts my sister."

"I didn't think you were." He leaned forward, resting his elbows on the table. "But you don't need to worry. Carse has been all about Carolyn since the moment he saw her."

Kimi studied him. "What about you?"

"What about me?"

"Did you have your eye on my sister too? And Carson beat you to the punch in asking Carolyn out?"

"Why would you say that?"

"Because my sister is very pretty."

Cal reached out and smoothed one of Kimi's curls behind her ear. "Must run in the family. She ain't got nothin' on you, Kimi West."

She didn't so much as crack a smile. But she didn't push his hand away either. "Carolyn's a good girl."

"I'm sure she is. She's good for Carson. He needs a woman like her to balance out his wildness. Carolyn seems to understand the kind of man he is."

"That she does. And she's marrying him anyway."

Cal fought a frown.

"Are you as wild as your twin, Calvin McKay?"

"Why? You lookin' for that?"

Kimi's answering smile hit the mark between sweet and sly.

That grin did funny things to him. He needed to feel that smile against his lips. "What are your plans while you're here?"

"None besides getting my sister married off. Even after only bein' here a few hours I'm happy me'n my aunt leave the day after the wedding."

"Why? Aren't you glad to be home?"

Kimi shook her head and sadness filled her eyes. "Wyoming doesn't feel like home."

"But Montana does?"

"No. I'd rather be there than here, though."

"Why? Isn't your school like a nunnery?"

"Yeah. But I know what to expect there. I know what to expect when I'm living with my aunt. Here...I walk on eggshells from the moment I step into the house. And it'll make me sound like a brat, but I hate that when I'm here, I'm supposed to just keep my mouth shut and do as I'm told."

Cal watched as she finished her ice cream, wishing they could get back to the easy way they'd started out. After she wiped her mouth, he reached for her hand. "Since Carson already broke the rules by fallin' for a West, it probably won't be as big a deal if I take you out while you're here."

"You'd knock on the front door, look my dad in the eye and tell him you're there for me?"

"Yep."

"While that is bold as brass, and I appreciate you bein' willing to get the shit kicked out of you, that can't happen, Calvin."

The breathy way she drew out his name was sexy as all get-out. It nearly escaped his notice that she'd said...no. His eyes narrowed. "You turnin' me down, darlin'?"

She placed her small hand over the top of his and traced the rough edges of his knuckles. "Good lord. Look at how big your hands are." Then she trailed her fingers over the back of his hand and up his forearm. "How do you get such ropy muscles?"

Since she'd touched him first, Cal cupped her cheek with his other hand, tilting her face up to meet his gaze. "Answer the question, Kimi."

Looking completely flustered, she said, "Can you repeat it?"

"Will you go out with me?"

"I suppose... But you can't pick me up at my parents' house."

While he waited for further explanation, he feathered his thumb across her cheekbone. "Why not?"

"Carolyn is an adult so there's nothin' my folks could've done about her dating a McKay. I, on the other hand, am *not* of legal age, so they can keep me from seein' you." She smirked. "If they find out about it."

"So you're sayin'…?"

"I'll go out with you, but only if we can meet someplace."

Cal wasn't the type to sneak around. But as he looked at her, touched her, he knew he'd break all the rules for the chance to spend time with her. "I'll agree, if you're sure there's no other way."

Kimi's gaze roamed over his face. Whatever she saw made her smile and Cal felt like he'd passed a test. "There isn't any other option. So how about if we plan on doing something after the wedding? I'll have my mom's car and none of my family will question what I'm doin' on that day once the reception is done."

"Sounds like a date." He slid his hand down and outlined her lips with the pad of his thumb. "Fair warning, darlin'. I'm gonna have my mouth all over yours as soon as we're alone."

Her breath caught.

He murmured, "You ever been kissed?"

"Yes. Lots of times."

Jealousy speared his gut. "By school boys," he scoffed.

"So?" She attempted to retreat.

But Cal held steady, his gaze firmly focused on that pouty mouth of hers. "So get ready to understand the difference between havin' a boy kiss you and havin' a man devour you," he said with a gruff edge.

On the next pass of his thumb across the center of her lower lip, Kimi opened her mouth and sank her teeth into the knuckle below his thumbnail. Then she pulled his hand away from her face and returned it to the table. She leaned in. "Fair warning, darlin'," she mimicked, "I'm gonna expect a kiss that blows my hair back."

They were close enough that he could plant his mouth on hers and level her with a kiss so hot not only would it blow her hair back, it'd blow her skirt up too.

A shadow fell across the table.

"Break it up," Carson growled. "Come on, Cal, we gotta git."

Cal kissed the inside of Kimi's wrist before lowering her hand to the table. "See you Sunday, sweetheart."

"Keep the groom outta trouble," Kimi said to Cal without looking up at Carson. "No strip clubs. And he'd better not be hung over when he pledges his life to my sister or I'm holding you responsible, Calvin McKay."

Like he had any control over his wild brother. But Cal knew Carson would be on his best behavior—at least until Carolyn bore his last name. "I'll make sure of it."

Chapter Two

Holy crap.

Holy, holy crap.

After Cal and Carson walked out, Kimi kept it together. But her knees were still weak when she climbed into the car. She pulled out a cigarette and hoped her sister didn't notice how badly her hands shook as she struck the match. Besides, who'd believe one encounter with Calvin McKay had the power to affect her that profoundly? She wouldn't have believed it herself half an hour ago.

Carolyn slammed the door and turned to look at her accusingly.

As usual, Kimi bristled. "What?"

"What happened between you and Cal?"

"Nothin'." *Such a lie. I think the man just changed my life.* "We talked. Why?"

"Well, the phrase 'struck dumb' doesn't apply because Cal did more than stare at you and mumble. He was really forward."

"Forward?" Kimi snorted. "For godsake, Carolyn, you sound like Aunt Hulda. And maybe Cal's actions are a McKay thing since it sounds like Carson has been pretty *forward* with you."

"Don't try and change the subject. You two seemed to be having a flirting contest."

"Oh, there's no contest—Calvin McKay wins, hands down," she murmured.

"That's because he has a lot of experience."

Kimi drew in another lungful of smoke and exhaled. "Is this where you tell me he's too old for me?"

Carolyn sighed. "Will you get mad if I say yes?"

"Yeah, but I wanna hear your reasons why you think the man—who, at twenty-four, is *exactly* the same age as your fiancé—is too old for me."

"Because you're almost two years younger than me!"

"So?"

Her sister's hands tightened on the steering wheel. "So, have you spent time with guys who aren't high school students but have been out in the working world for several years?"

"You're kiddin' me, right? I barely ever get to see *any* guys, let alone get to shoot the breeze with them in an unchaperoned situation since I live in a convent most of the year."

"Were you serious at lunch? When you said you wanted to drop out of school?"

"No! I just like to tease Aunt Hulda since she's footing the bill for our *ed-ja-kay-shun*. Of course Mom took the opportunity to jump on me for it and call me ungrateful." It was just another indication that her mom had never understood her sense of humor—or anything else about her. "So don't you dare say anything to her about me flirting with Cal."

"I'd never do that." Carolyn said. "Did you know that Thomas tried to fix me up with one of his friends?"

"A coal miner?"

"No. A college guy."

"And?" Kimi prompted.

"And I'd already met Carson. I couldn't help but compare them. But there was no comparison. At all."

Kimi thought back to Cal's sexy taunt. *Get ready to understand the difference between havin' a boy kiss you and havin' a man devour you.* "How do you think Cal compares? Bein's he and Carson are twins?"

"I don't know Cal well. Yet. But even in the short amount of time I've spent with him, I've found him to be more introspective. He doesn't seem prone to the same impulsive behavior that Carson deals with."

"So Cal isn't a brawler?"

"Only if he's backing his fight-lovin' twin," Carolyn said dryly.

"Well, I appreciate the concern, sis, but Cal is outta my league." She sighed. "That's not to say I can't admire him and practice my flirting skills because he's so good lookin'. Lord, his smile just lights up that whole handsome face of his. And those blue eyes..."

"They're something, aren't they? The whole McKay family has that eye color."

"Maybe all your babies will too," Kimi teased.

Carolyn blushed. But she didn't say anything else.

After taking one last drag of her cigarette, Kimi flicked the butt out the window. The scenery flew by. Nothing changed here. The desolate landscape depressed her. It always had.

Aside from Carolyn's giddiness about her husband-to-be, it shocked Kimi that her sister had signed on to live in the vast void of Wyoming for the rest of her life. They'd both talked of getting out. Moving on. Kimi had selfishly hoped Carolyn would move to Chicago with her friend Cathy. Then she'd have a place to go when she finished her sentence at St. Mary's, because there was no way in hell she was ever coming back here. No way.

One more year. She could survive that. She'd taken extra classes the past two years so she could graduate a year early—not that anyone in her family besides Aunt Hulda was aware of her plans. Catholic school had been tolerable with Carolyn around as a buffer. Everyone adored her big sister and that admiration had provided Kimi with a layer of protection from the holier-than-thou girls populating the school. Now that Carolyn had graduated, the torture had already begun for Kimi during her summer classes.

She hated her classmates' judgment and supposition. They called her a fast girl just because she paid attention to the opposite sex when she had the chance. Kimi wasn't fast or loose—as evidenced by her virginal status. But just to entertain herself, she'd adopted the attitude of a wild child. Let her classmates whisper and talk about her. It amused her that her only transgression had been detention for getting caught smoking.

"Kimi? You all right?"

She tamped down her melancholy. "I'm just tired." She dreaded being left alone with her mom and dad while Carolyn and Aunt Hulda worked on the wedding dress. But she'd sworn not to cause any family problems. Her sister had enough to deal with. "This will be a quick trip for us."

"Does that mean you won't see any of your friends while you're here?"

"What friends? I've been livin' in Montana for six years. That's longer than I went to school around here."

"I recognize that disjointed feeling," Carolyn said softly. "Like you don't belong here and you don't belong there."

That startled Kimi. Carolyn never said things like that. She always looked on the bright side of everything.

"But Carson changed that," Carolyn said.

"How so?"

"Now I know exactly where I belong. With him."

Kimi reached over and squeezed Carolyn's knee. "You are such a sap. Are you gonna cry during the wedding ceremony?"

"Probably."

"Then I'll make sure to tuck some extra tissues into my bra."

Carolyn lifted one brow. "Extra? How is that different from how you dress every day?"

"Hey! I've never stuffed my bra!" Kimi cupped her breasts and lifted them up. "No need to. More than a handful is a waste." She paused thoughtfully. "Or do guys say more than a mouthful is a waste?"

"Good lord, Kimi."

She laughed. "You started it." She cranked up the radio. By the time the chorus to "California Dreamin'" started they were both singing along. She let her worries float away and embraced these last few days with her sister before both their lives changed.

Kimi decided sitting in silence in the sun porch while Carolyn and Aunt Hulda sewed the wedding dress was a far sight better than being berated by her father as he sat in front of the TV.

No surprise he hadn't given her a hug when he'd seen her, even when it'd been eight months since she'd been back here. Sometimes she wondered how her mom had gotten pregnant so many times when her father never showed her—or anyone else—the slightest bit of affection.

Her brothers didn't say much to her—they mostly steered clear of the uncomfortable situation.

Carolyn got up early Sunday morning to make the entire family breakfast, even though it was her wedding day. Aunt Hulda huffed about it but didn't say anything when her nephews scarfed down the food with scarcely a thanks and walked away from the table.

Kimi shooed Carolyn out of the kitchen, telling her to get ready while she tackled the dishes. She needed a moment alone to get a handle on her anger. This family expected so much from Carolyn—and Kimi when she was here—but gave so little in return.

One more day. Thankfully she had her date with Cal McKay to look forward to tonight. Part of her had wanted to tell her father about it after he'd started spewing crap about the McKays last night. Part of her had wanted to ask her mother what was wrong with her for saying nothing in defense of her daughter's future husband. But she knew it'd be a waste of breath. Plus, it'd make things worse for her sister, since Caro believed their mother had stood up to their father, when in actuality, she'd just shut up. Kimi's responsibility as Carolyn's maid of honor was to manage the stress and drama so the bride could focus entirely on the happiest day of her life.

Her brother Thomas walked into the kitchen as she wiped down the last counter. Perfect timing; right when she'd finished.

He leaned against the wall and studied her.

"What do you want?" Kimi demanded.

"Why are you so defensive?"

"It's a habit, ingrained from the years I lived here. Besides, you can't blame me for bein' suspicious. You never track me down just to talk."

"That's true. And I am sorry about that, Kimi. I guess that's why I was hoping you'd stick around the rest of the summer. We could talk and stuff."

Kimi draped the rag over the edge of the sink and squared off against her brother. "It's the 'stuff' part that bothers me, Thomas."

"Why?"

"Because I'm pissed off that you, Stuart and Marshall manage to do all the household *stuff* during the rest of the year when Carolyn and I aren't here. But the second we're back, you guys turn into Dad."

"You calling us lazy?"

"No, I'm calling you selfish."

Thomas scowled. "You should talk. And you're making a lot of assumptions that you'll have a choice in this *stuff* that happens next."

"What's that mean?"

"Look, we both know Dad won't show up at the wedding. He's already left the house and gone to Harland's."

Their oldest brother and their dad were best buds, which is why she didn't get along with Harland. "That's not a surprise. So?"

Worry clouded his eyes. "So Carolyn is really okay with me giving her away?"

"Yes. I know she's grateful that one of her brothers is happy for her."

"I am." He jammed his hand through his hair. "I hate this shit, Kimi. I really do. It eats at all of us."

She didn't say, *it eating at you hasn't affected any of your appetites.*

"Anyway, what's the plan for getting everyone to the church?"

"I'll drive Carolyn early so she can get ready. I assumed Aunt Hulda would drive Mom there and then back here afterward. And you, Stuart and Marshall would ride together. Why?"

"Just wondered how long this would last."

Her brothers rarely went to church. "It's a typical Catholic ceremony without mass. So probably forty-five minutes. Since there's so few people invited to the wedding I doubt the reception will last long." She smirked. "I'm sure the bride and groom are anxious to get to the honeymoon portion of the day."

Thomas returned her smirk. "I imagine they are. What are your plans for after the ceremony?"

She shrugged. "I'm playing it by ear."

"Let me offer you some advice, little sis. Stay away from here until later tonight."

Not what she'd expected. "Why?"

"Dad will come home from Harland's drunk. I suspect it'll be worse than usual due to Carolyn's marriage. He'll rant and rave at anyone who's around until he passes out. I plan to be elsewhere, as do Stuart and Marshall."

"Thanks for the warning." She pushed away from the counter. "I should get myself ready and see how the bride is doin'."

When she stood in the entryway to the sun porch, seeing Carolyn's suitcase packed and waiting by the door, it finally hit her that this was it. Last night was the last time they'd share the same space as they talked of their hopes for the future and their favorite moments from their past.

Carolyn looked over at her. "What's wrong?"

Emotion overwhelmed her and her tears fell. "You are beautiful. Carson might faint dead away when he gets a look at you."

Her sister blushed. Then she lifted her chin. "I appreciate the flattery, Kimi, but what's really going on? You're not usually a crier."

Yesterday they'd moved all of Carolyn's things into Carson's trailer. She'd fussed and cleaned. Rearranged and added decorative touches, turning the place from his space into their space. Kimi had watched her sister flitting around, feeling a mixture of envy and repulsion. Envy because Carolyn had found a man who loved her for her. Repulsion because it seemed like her sister was settling down too soon. Carolyn wouldn't get to do interesting things or travel to fascinating places. She worried her sister's life would be just as mundane living in Carson's house as it had been living in their parent's house.

Aren't you projecting your goals onto her? Has Carolyn ever told you that she wants to travel?

No.

But now it wasn't an option for her. And that was a little sad.

"Kimi?" Carolyn prompted.

Her gaze snapped to her sister. "Sorry. It's a lot to take in. It's weird seeing all your stuff packed up."

"More room for you to spread out when you come home." Carolyn added another coat of mascara on her already ridiculously long eyelashes. "I pushed the beds back together for you."

"Thanks. Since no one is in the bathroom, I'll grab my stuff and get ready."

Kimi planned to wear her hair up. Since she couldn't find any bobby pins, she'd borrow some from her mother. She stopped outside her mom's bedroom door when she heard her name uttered angrily.

"Kimi doesn't want to return to school, Hulda. You heard her."

"She was joking, Clara, and it proves that you don't really listen to her. Besides, I wouldn't *let* her drop out."

"That is *not* for you to decide," her mother snapped. "Kimi is *not* your daughter."

What a nasty thing for her mom to say.

"I love her and Carolyn like they *are* mine," her aunt said proudly. "I'll never apologize for that. I'll never apologize for giving them options."

Kimi closed her eyes, but she couldn't force herself to walk away.

"I know you love them. I just didn't expect you'd take them from me," her mother said on a sob. "I wanted you to help them, not turn them into strangers and turn them against me."

"Oh, quit sniveling. I haven't done any such thing and you know it. You stopped being a mother to them when you sent them away, even when you did it for their own good. Kimi's been on her own longer than Carolyn. She comes home and doesn't understand why all the work burden falls on Carolyn's shoulders or hers, knowing when they aren't here, their brothers manage just fine. So no, I don't care what that husband of yours says—Kimi is *not* staying here as a fill-in servant. I need Kimi at the shop. Plus, she's already missing two days of the summer session and she'll have plenty of homework to catch up on when we return."

"Elijah is her father. He has a say in what happens to his youngest daughter."

No he doesn't.

"We'll discuss this later." The chair creaked, indicating her aunt had gotten up.

Kimi recognized Aunt Hulda's stalling technique, so she retreated to the bathroom, bobby pins forgotten.

As she fixed her hair she wondered why her mother was pushing so hard to keep her here, when just Friday afternoon she'd pointed out that Kimi had no choice but to stay in school since her aunt was paying for it. Was it just a control thing? Letting her sister and her daughter know she could upend both their lives any time she chose?

Like hell that'd ever happen. She'd run away first.

Three sharp knocks sounded on the door. "Kimi? You about ready?" Carolyn asked.

"Give me two more minutes and then we'll go."

Kimi pressed a hand to her stomach. She had butterflies, which didn't make sense since she wasn't the one getting married.

But it was her job to get the bride to the church on time.

Chapter Three

The wedding was short and sweet—except for the passionate kiss Carson laid on Carolyn as soon as the priest pronounced them husband and wife.

Kimi's eyes had met Cal's across the altar and they grinned at each other.

That'd been the only time during the ceremony Kimi had allowed her eyes to stray to the too-handsome cowboy, looking fine in a navy-colored western-cut suit. She'd known if she didn't pay attention to the priest, she'd get lost in Cal's eyes and remember nothing of the ceremony.

While Mr. and Mrs. McKay greeted their guests downstairs at the reception, Kimi and Cal signed the marriage license in the priest's office. Cal acted circumspect while the priest was around, but the minute the holy man left...holy crap did Cal's eyes roam over every inch of her.

At least twice.

He murmured, "Lookin' good, little sister," in her ear and gooseflesh broke out across her arms.

By unspoken agreement they didn't acknowledge one another during the reception. He stayed with the McKay guests; she stayed with the West guests.

Then Cal snagged her attention and they met in the middle of the room, where she swore she felt all eyes on them. "I need to get Carolyn's stuff transferred into Carson's truck. You wanna give me your car keys?"

"You afraid tongues will wag if we head outside together?"

"No, darlin', I'm afraid fists will fly."

He had a point. "The suitcase is in the trunk. I didn't lock the car since the lock always sticks."

"I'll still need the keys."

She fished them out of her purse and handed them over.

"I'll be movin' Carson's truck out front so maybe it's time to gather everyone out there for the sendoff."

Kimi approached her family. Four of her bothers had attended: Darren, Marshall, Stuart, Thomas. Harland hadn't shown up, but his wife Sonia had, as well as Darren's wife, Tracy.

Darren spoke first. "What'd that other McKay want?"

"To know where to find Carolyn's things before we send the newlyweds off." She looked at her aunt. "It's about time to throw rice. Maybe you'd better get Mom into position outside."

"Where will you be?" her mother demanded.

"Fulfilling my maid of honor duties," she said evenly.

A quick pit stop in the kitchen assured Kimi that the ladies' auxiliary had packaged up the leftover German chocolate butter cake Aunt Hulda had made. Kimi grabbed the coffee can filled with rice, passing off the duty of handing out rice to her sister-in-law, Sonia.

The priest was chatting with the newlyweds. Carson looked anxious—but so did Carolyn. Cal caught Kimi's eye and smiled before interrupting the priest.

"Carse, your truck is parked at the curb and loaded with your wife's things, so you're all set."

Carson kissed Carolyn's forehead. "Let's go home."

After exchanging a hug with her sister and new brother-in-law, Kimi opened the doors. Carson and Carolyn raced through a hail of rice. That bone-deep sadness reared its ugly head again. She knew being jealous was stupid, because she was happy for her sister, but the one person who tied her to this family...would now have a family of her own. It'd always been her and Carolyn facing the world. The West sisters standing up for each other, protecting one another, inside the family and outside.

She'd never felt so alone.

No one noticed Kimi sneaking back into the church. Around the corner in the sanctuary, she pressed her back against the brick wall and let the tears come full force—but in silence.

Not long after she disappeared, a shadow fell over her. "Aw, hell, sweet darlin'. Those tears are killin' me. C'mere." Cal's strong arm slipped around her waist. A solid chest cushioned her cheek and muffled her sobs. A gentle hand skated up and down her back.

She accepted his comfort without question.

He said nothing, he just held her until she calmed down.

"I didn't mean to lose it," she whispered.

"You didn't. Not like you could have—throwin' shit, screamin' obscenities and swigging from a bottle of whiskey."

"There's plenty of day left for that."

"And ain't I the lucky one, for getting to spend the rest of it with you."

She managed a hiccupping laugh. "You sure you still want to do that?"

"Yep. More than anything in the world, actually."

Kimi finally looked up at him. Butterflies took wing in her stomach again. This man was...all man.

Cal curled his hand around her cheek. "You are a little whip of a thing."

"I've got a chip on my shoulder about that, so watch it. I'm small but mighty."

His lips twitched. "Thanks for the warning. So I thought you could come over to my place."

His place? Like it was no big deal if she was alone, with a man, at his house? She'd never imagined that's where they'd end up on this "date". Since they were in a church, she felt the need to confess the truth. "I'm not a wild girl, Cal."

He lifted both eyebrows. "You're tellin' me this...why?"

"I've been told I flirt too much, so I might've given you the wrong impression." She tried to squirm away but he held tight.

His blue eyes were hard as steel. "Seems you've been listening to your family run down the McKays. You assume I'm the type of man who'd take advantage of you?"

Kimi didn't back down. "That's the thing—I don't know *what* kind of man you are. I'm just letting you know what kind of girl I'm *not*. So if you want to change your mind..."

"I don't." He touched her cheek. "I ain't gonna lie, Kimi. There's a pull between us. But acknowledging it and actin' on it are two different things. I just want to get to know you."

"So this isn't really a date?"

He shrugged. "Call it whatever makes you comfortable. But I promise I won't try and talk you into my bed."

"Okay. Thank you for bein'..."

"For bein' what, sweet darlin'?"

A sudden burst of shyness had her dropping her gaze. "For bein' cool about the fact I'm not cool. That I'm just a dorky teenage girl who has no idea what I've gotten myself into with you."

Cal chuckled. "You're makin' me feel old."

She looked up at him. "Will you take offense if I say you seem older than twenty-four?"

"Not if you don't take offense if I say you seem older than sixteen."

She smiled.

His returning grin was decidedly boyish.

She liked his charming side. She really liked that he knew when to use it and when to rein it in.

"We'll wait until everyone leaves and then you can follow me. It's about an hour drive. So if you're hungry we should stop and eat first."

"I'm starved."

Cal kissed her forehead. Then he stepped back. "Wait here. I'll see if the coast is clear."

Kimi rested her shoulders against the wall and breathed a sigh of relief. With him, she wouldn't have to pretend to be something she wasn't.

Both Cal and Kimi were surprised they'd lingered at the diner for an hour after they finished their meals.

During the drive to his house, he kept checking his rearview mirror—almost obsessively—to make sure she followed him, because he knew he'd chase her down if she turned around.

Even after only spending about three hours with Kimi, Cal was crazy about her. They'd had an instant connection—despite their age difference, despite their warring families, despite the fact they shouldn't have anything in common besides that their siblings had gotten married.

But they had similar tastes and opinions. He knew it sounded stupid, but she made him feel young—or, more accurately, closer to his own age.

Sometimes Cal felt like an old man in a young man's body. In addition to his growing ranch responsibilities, he'd been mediating between Carson and their dad for years, as well as Carson and their brothers. Cal rarely went looking for a fight, but he'd been in more than his fair share of them because Carson liked to mix it up and he always had his brother's back.

Most days being part of the "McKay twins" moniker didn't bother Cal. For the first few years after they'd moved into their own place, he'd even been happy with Carson's cast-off conquests. Carson had earned his love-'em-and-leave-'em reputation for a reason; he wasn't interested in anything besides a one-time fuck. It never made sense to Cal, why these same women turned to him—the supposed "good" twin—after they'd already been dumped by his brother. For all he knew they showed up at the trailer hoping to get double-teamed by the McKay twins, which was really fucking creepy. But Cal wasn't an idiot. If free, easy pussy was offered? He'd take it. He just had more tact than his brother when it came to letting the ladies know he wasn't interested in anything serious.

But he suspected local single women would be dropping by with "housewarming" meals in the hopes that he'd be more open to settling down now that Carson had gotten married.

Like hell.

Cal shoved those thoughts aside and watched Kimi park behind his truck. He opened the driver's side door of her car and offered her his hand to help her out. "I just had a load of gravel dumped here yesterday, so watch your step."

She scowled at the powdery orange dirt beneath her feet. "So much for my white shoes."

Grinning, he scooped her into his arms, carried her to the cement stoop and set her down. "Better?"

"Why, thank you, kind sir, for rescuing my shoes from certain death," she said in a southern drawl.

"No problem, little lady. Need anything else outta the car?"

"There's a traveling case in the back seat."

Cal grabbed the suitcase and brought it to her. "Whatcha got in there?"

"A change of clothes."

He slipped his finger under the collar of his shirt. "I don't remember the last time I wore a suit, but I remember why I don't like 'em." He tugged at the ends of his tie until it loosened. "Felt like I was choking."

Kimi stepped forward and smoothed her hands down his lapels. "You sure look good though. You oughta wear these all the time."

Her casual touch tightened the muscles in his belly. "Thanks." He kept his left hand resting on the small of her back when he reached over to open the front door. "Ladies first."

"You don't lock your door?"

"Nothin' in here worth stealing." When Kimi stopped just inside the entryway, Cal had a bout of nerves. "Place is a mess bein's I just moved in."

"I remember Carolyn telling me you lived with Carson up until they set a wedding date."

"We bought this place recently and it wouldn't have been done in time for the newlyweds to move in so he passed it off to me."

She wandered into the living room. "There's a lot of room for a bachelor."

"Tell me about it. There's an entire upper level, that's been closed off, I haven't even thought about. I'm just happy we put on a new roof in the main part of the house and fixed the windows."

Kimi looked over her shoulder at him. "You don't have any furniture?"

"Just a table and chairs in the kitchen. And a bed and dresser in my room."

"No TV?"

"Not yet."

"Whatever will we do tonight, Mr. McKay?"

Cal could name half a dozen things he'd rather do with her than watch TV. "Got a porch swing out back."

"That sounds heavenly." She looked around. "Where can I change?"

"The bathroom is the first door on the left down the hall."

She picked up her suitcase.

After the bathroom door closed, Cal hustled to his room and kicked aside his pile of dirty clothes as he shed his suit jacket, tie, vest and long-sleeved white shirt. Off came his dress boots and suit pants. He pulled on his last clean pair of jeans. Since all his shirts were dirty, he'd be stuck wearing an undershirt, which always made him feel half-naked.

Leaning against the wall, he shoved his foot into his work boot, eyeing his bedroom with disgust. He hadn't made his bed this morning. Heck, he hadn't bought a bedframe yet; the mattress was still on the floor. Carson had always given him crap about being a neatnik, but Cal had decided early on that being a bachelor didn't mean he had to live in a pigsty. In the past week he'd dropped into bed with such exhaustion that he'd awoken twice to see he still had his work clothes and boots on. So his room being a disaster was a blessing in disguise—he wouldn't be tempted to bring Kimi in here.

He shut his bedroom door at the same moment Kimi exited the bathroom. She wore the shorts and blouse he'd seen her in the first time they'd met. How was he supposed to keep his hands off her tight little ass? And off those surprisingly long legs, so perfectly proportioned in such a petite package?

Cal was beginning to think this was a bad, bad idea.

"Cal?" she said softly.

His gaze moved up her body, lingering on the swell of her breasts, before his eyes met hers. "Would you like a drink?"

"Sure. What do you have?"

Dammit. She wasn't old enough for booze. "Root beer or milk."

A heavy pause followed. "Milk? Really?" Her eyes flashed. "Well, *Daddy*, I want cookies and a bedtime story if you intend to treat me like a child."

He bridged the distance between them with two steps. He traced the edge of her defiant jaw with the backs of his knuckles. "Sweet darlin', I'm fully aware you ain't a child. But I also know you've gotta drive home so you need to stay away from booze. So how about that root beer?"

"You having one?"

"Nope. I'm home for the night." He stepped away and opened the refrigerator. He pried off the cap before handing over the bottle of root beer. Then he snagged a glass from the cupboard and poured himself three fingers of Jack Daniels.

"Whiskey straight up? Not even on ice?"

"I don't have ice. And I never saw the point of diluting whiskey. If I wanted to taste water, that's what I'd drink."

"That's what my Aunt Hulda says too. She lets me have a nip of hers now and then. Although she prefers Irish whiskey to American."

"So does Carson. He got that from our dad."

"What about your brothers?"

"Casper drinks whatever is cheapest. Charlie isn't much of a drinker, but he's young."

Charlie is older than Kimi, his conscience chose to point out.

Kimi held her bottle of soda aloft. "To the happy couple. May the good times outweigh the bad."

Strange toast, but he touched his glass to hers anyway and said, "Amen," before taking a sip.

"So show me this porch swing. It's not something I expected a bachelor to have."

Cal took her hand, leading her through the kitchen and out the back door. "It came with the house."

Kimi stopped on the edge of the cement patio. "Cal. This is so cool."

The brick house had been built after the First World War. It wasn't like other houses in rural Wyoming and he'd been secretly glad that Carson had given it over to him so easily. The entire area behind the house, half an acre deep, was ringed with lilac bushes that created a natural fence. The grass back here wasn't the weed-like variety that surrounded the trailer, but thicker and softer like the manicured lawns in town. Although water was scarce, the man who'd owned the place had rigged up a windmill and pump that hooked into an irrigation system. None of it currently worked but once things slowed down the next couple of weeks, Cal planned on fixing it. "You like it?"

"I love it. It's an oasis in the desert." She pointed to the raised areas sectioned off with old railroad ties. "Are all of those flower beds?"

"I guess some were vegetable gardens. The man we bought it from said he'd let everything go after his wife died because it was too hard to be out here in her domain without her. Even seeing it now, I imagine this place was really something."

Kimi got right in his face. "Promise me you'll take care of it and get it back to the way it used to be. Even if you have to ask Carolyn to help you. She knows a lot about flowers and gardening."

"Maybe I don't want her to see it, so she won't get it in her head that she wants to move in, and I'll be back in the trailer," he retorted.

She laughed. But then she grew somber. "You're serious, aren't you?"

Cal sipped his whiskey. "Yep. I've never had anything that was just mine. Carson and Dad were more interested in the Ag land to give the house and the barn more than a passing glance. They saw a sagging roof, busted windows and space that'd become a critter habitat. I saw more." Why had he admitted that? And how did he know Kimi wouldn't blab all this to her sister the second she got the chance?

But she was intuitive. Her gaze softened. "I promise your secret garden is safe with me, Cal McKay." She tugged on his hand. "Let's sit on the swing and you can tell me all about your plans for this place, because I know you've got them."

Nosy little thing. But he was amused by her insistence rather than annoyed. After they'd settled in the swing, she asked a million questions, offered suggestions and generally entertained the hell out of him. She was sweet and funny and real.

Talk shifted to their families. Kimi spoke of her mother's health problems with detachment, but Cal didn't blame her. It sounded as if there'd been a disconnect between mother and youngest daughter for more than half of Kimi's life. She said even less about her father. She did talk about her brothers, and seemed both resigned and grateful that she wasn't closer to them.

"What about your mom?" she prompted.

"She died suddenly when me'n Carse were eighteen. Dad turned his grief into anger and somehow that ended up aimed at us."

"That stinks."

"Yeah. I guess Dad didn't consider that we'd lost something too. After six months of dealin' with that shit, Carson decided we needed to move out on our own."

The chains on the swing creaked as they set it to moving again.

"We?" she asked.

"Yep. The McKay twins are a matched set."

"Do you do everything your brother wants?" Right after Kimi said it, she tensed, as if she expected him to bristle.

"Usually. Not because I ain't got a backbone or my own opinion, but because he's usually right. Our dad might be in charge, but Carson sees the whole picture. What's important now and how it'll change years down the road. I ain't gonna argue with him just to show my ignorance like our brother Casper does. But if Carson is in the wrong, I ain't afraid to tell him so."

"You two don't have problems? Get into fistfights? Refuse to talk to one another?"

He shrugged. "Not really. At least not about ranch stuff. Some folks think I oughta have resentment for Carson bein' in charge when he's just a few minutes older. But the truth is, I'd defer to him even if I was a few *years* older. His gut feeling ain't ever been wrong. And that makes it easier on me, to be honest. Not everyone is cut out to give orders." He took another drink of whiskey, surprised to see it was gone. He'd been pacing himself and by his count they'd been out here two hours.

"I know what you mean. At the shop, Carolyn takes the initiative in creating new styles and she loves all aspects of sewing. Whereas I... It doesn't interest me. I mean, I'm competent. I do what I'm told with no problem, but Aunt Hulda accepts my limitations. She doesn't expect me to be exactly like Carolyn. But when I come back here, that's the only expectation everyone else in my family has—why can't you be more like Carolyn?" Kimi drained her root beer. She plucked his glass out of his hand and gently set both empties in the grass.

Cal dropped his arm over her shoulder and stroked her soft skin. "So does that mean now that Carolyn's married off...you're just bidin' your time until you can do the same so you don't disappoint your family?"

Kimi snorted at his teasing tone. "Not likely. I could ask you the same question. You'n Carson have lived together and worked together your whole lives. You got resentment for havin' to share your brother with my sister? Or maybe you'll get married soon so you and the missus can do couple things with the Carson McKays."

He put his lips on her ear. "Maybe *you* oughta marry me. At least I know you'd get along with your sister-in-law." Once again her scent, a powdery sweetness with an underlying hint of smoke teased his nose.

She trembled as he breathed her in.

It wasn't enough. He wanted to taste her mouth. Feel the gooseflesh rippling across her skin beneath his lips. "Kimi. Darlin', look at me."

She tipped her head back and turned her face toward his, keeping her cheek nestled against his biceps. "What?"

"I wanna kiss you. Christ, girl, I wanna eat you up. Then I remember you're young and I oughten be entertaining those kinda thoughts at all. And I promised—"

Kimi put her finger over his lips. "You promised not to try and get me in bed. But you didn't say a damn thing about not tryin' to kiss me. In fact, you promised you were gonna have your mouth all over mine, remember?"

Without missing a beat, Cal planted his mouth on hers very softly, almost chastely, giving her a chance to pull away.

So when she parted her lips and arched up, pressing her chest to his, he groaned and forced himself to explore her, not devour her like his body demanded.

Her mouth tasted sweet—a bit of root beer lingered on her lips and he delicately licked it away. He tested how she reacted to each soft smooch, each tender nibble, each exploring flick of his tongue.

When Kimi tired of his slower pace, she dug her nails into the back of his neck, and pulled him forward, opening her mouth wider beneath his. Thrusting her tongue in to stroke, twirl and tangle. To drive him out of his fucking mind.

From just a kiss.

Cal couldn't remember the last time he'd kissed a woman with no agenda beyond learning the shape of her mouth as it moved beneath his. Experiencing the unique flavor of her. Exchanging breath as the hunger expanded. Feeling her blood pulsing in her lips. Each kiss drove the need higher until he couldn't think. Until his heartbeat thundered in his ears, in his chest, in his cock.

A sharp pain forced him to ease back, changing the tenor of the kiss from sizzling hot to sweetly warm.

He smiled when she chased his mouth, demanding more. "I'm not nearly done with you, but there's a crick in my neck so I've gotta move."

Then shy, inexperienced Kimi disappeared and she shifted to straddle his lap, with her knees touching the back of the swing. They were face to face. Mouth to mouth. She kept her eyes on his as she followed the contours of his shoulders to his neck with her hands. She swept her thumbs over the section of skin between his jaw and his earlobe. Then her gaze zeroed in on his mouth. "Can I tell you something?"

Please tell me that you're really eighteen and I can do all the dirty things to you I've been dreaming up since I saw you lick that ice cream cone. "Sure."

"You were right."

"About?"

"I've never been kissed like that."

Cal curled his hands around her hips and squeezed. "You want more of them lip-melting kisses, darlin'?"

She whispered, "God, yes," and affixed her mouth to his, her lips parted in invitation, but she paused, waiting to let him lead.

This time he drew out the pleasure. This time his hands didn't stay idle. He ran his palms down her strong back, across her surprisingly muscular arms, up her taut thighs, around to squeeze her lush ass and then back to cradle her head, all the while feeling the softness of her hair across his knuckles as he touched her.

And fuck if he didn't love the sexy sounds she made when he did something she wasn't expecting. Like the first time he trailed his lips down her throat and sucked on the spot where her neck met her shoulder.

Her surprised, throaty gasp tightened his balls.

Kimi's hands went from clutching his neck, to pulling his hair, to unconsciously pushing his head where she wanted his mouth.

Cal kept his hands away from her breasts and avoided touching her between her thighs. But when her body figured out what to do and she started grinding on him, he backed off immediately, before he lost the ability to do so.

"Kimi," he rasped against her throat, "time out."

"Okay." She swallowed hard. "Now I understand when people say they got carried away. It's never been like that for me before."

Don't tell her it gets even better than that.

She shifted and moved off his lap, giving his cock some relief. She rested her cheek against his chest, tucking the top of her head beneath his chin. "Is it weird if I just wanna stay like this for a while?"

"Not weird at all, darlin'." He swept his hand up her back. "Although I wish I had a couch we could stretch out on."

"Next time." She yawned. "I'm tired. It's been exhausting dealing with my family the past couple of days."

"I'll bet. Go ahead and close your eyes for a bit." He kissed her forehead.

As Kimi fell asleep in his arms he couldn't remember the last time he'd felt so content.

Chapter Four

Kimi woke up with a jolt, surrounded by darkness and heat. Warm, hard, delicious-smelling heat.

Soft lips brushed over her forehead. "Hey, sleepyhead."

God. She loved the deep rasp of Cal's voice. And the way his breath stole across her skin stirred something deep inside her. Everything about him was so...manly. Even the way he'd put the brakes on when things had gotten too hot between them. None of the boys she'd messed around with before had that kind of control. They got pissed if she said stop, or slow down, and were especially angry if she said no. Then they called her a cock tease or lied and told everyone that she'd done slutty things. Being with Cal the last few hours really drove home the difference between boys and real men. And not just in the way they kissed.

She rubbed her mouth across the soft cotton of his T-shirt and breathed in the heady scent of his body. "Sorry I conked out."

"No worries. I liked it enough that I fell asleep too."

"How long was I out?"

"An hour, hour and a half."

Kimi pushed herself away from him and turned so her legs dangled off the swing. She snickered. "I'm so damn short that my feet don't touch the ground."

Cal's hand skated down her arm. "I like that you're pint-sized. And darlin', you may be short, but you've got great gams."

Most guys were so busy staring at her chest they didn't see any part of her beyond that. And how charming was it that he didn't make his compliment crude? "Thanks." She hopped off the swing and faced him, holding out her hands to help him up from the swing.

A wolfish grin lit his face before he took her hands and pulled her right back onto his lap. Then he kissed her with sweet surety. "Thank you, Kimi, for comin' over. This is one of the best nights I can remember."

"You don't get out much, do you?" she teased.

"I get out more than you know, but it don't change nothin'. I meant it. And if you lived around here, I'd ask you to come over tomorrow too."

Kimi arched up to kiss him. "If I lived around here, I'd be over so often you might as well ask me to move in with you."

He laughed. "Oh, Eli West would have me arrested for sure for corrupting his underage daughter."

"Like you said to Carolyn, Cal...I'm not gonna be sixteen forever. In fact, I'll be seventeen next week."

"Happy Birthday. Maybe I oughta give you a birthday spankin' before you go."

"Save it for next time."

Cal's eyes searched hers. "There'll be a next time?"

"Yeah. Next time I'm around here." She trailed her fingers down his jaw. "You think it's weird that I feel like I've known you more than two days?"

"It'd make me weird too, then, 'cause I feel the same way."

"I like you, Cal McKay. A lot." Crap. Why had she said that? She probably sounded like a love-struck teen.

Aren't you?

He gave her a sexy smile that made her pulse race. "I like you a lot too, Kimi West. So you'd better call me when you come back for Christmas break."

"Really?"

"Yeah, sweet darlin'. I'd like that more than you know."

"I will." Kimi forced herself to move or she might stay right there, lost in his blue eyes forever. "I have to go."

"I know."

Cal carried her bag to the car. Then he gifted her with a kiss that could only be described as devastating.

When she pulled onto the road, she noticed he stood at the end of the driveway, watching her go.

Kimi tried to be as quiet as possible when she entered the house.

But she needn't have bothered since her dad had pulled over the easy chair and parked it in front of the door.

"Where in the hell have you been?" her father demanded. "It's almost midnight."

It took everything inside her not to cower and revert to that small child who was fearful of Daddy. "Out with a friend."

"I don't know who in the hell you think you are, girlie, bein' 'out with a friend' until goddamned midnight, but you are sixteen years old. We have rules in this house."

"Which are? I've never been real clear on them because you seem to have one set of rules for your sons and one for your daughters."

"You watch that smart mouth," he snapped.

Don't react.

"Things are gonna change around here. You will abide by *my* rules. As of right now, you're grounded. You're only allowed to go to the store."

Kimi squinted at him. How drunk was he? She should've let it go, but she wanted to point out that as of tomorrow he'd have no power over her. "You remember who you're talking to, right, Dad? It's Kimi. I'm goin' back to Billings tomorrow."

"Like hell you are. Now that your sister married that McKay bastard, I'll need you around here to take care of your mother and make sure that Carolyn doesn't turn against her family. We both know she won't cut us out if *you're* livin' here fulltime."

A slap in the face couldn't have hurt worse. They didn't want her here because they missed her. She balled her fists and said, "No."

Her dad stood. "No? You don't get to tell me *no*, little girl."

"Watch me." She shouted, "No, no, no, no, no!" at the top of her lungs. "I don't know how damn drunk you are, but I'm goin' back to St. Mary's to finish school."

"Wrong. As of tonight you'll finish out school here. You're running wild up there and I won't have it."

"Have you talked to Aunt Hulda about this?" she demanded.

He allowed a smug smile. "Don't gotta talk to her, bein's you're my kid, not hers, and I don't need her opinion."

"You can't do this."

"I think it's time you learn that I can."

Kimi cut around the chair and headed toward her mom's room.

"Get back here!" her dad bellowed.

She threw open the door and flipped on the lights.

Aunt Hulda sat up. "Kimi? What's going on?"

Kimi walked over to her mother's bed. Her eyes were open but she remained lying on her side. "Did you do this to spite me or to spite your sister?"

Her mother blinked and tried to turn her head away.

"Oh, no you don't. You've put your head in the sand way too long. And you're crazier than I thought you were if you think I'll stay here and coddle you and be a slave to him and my brothers since Carolyn was smart enough to get the hell out, or just because he says so."

"This is why we're not letting you go back to Billings, Kimberly."

"*Letting* me?" she shouted.

"What?" Aunt Hulda said from across the room.

"You need to be reminded whose family you belong to," her mother said with false bravado.

The bed creaked and then Aunt Hulda stood next to her. "Clara. What on earth are you talking about? Kimi is finishing out her education at St. Mary's."

"Not anymore, she ain't," her dad said behind her.

Kimi whirled around and faced him. "The only reason you want me here is so you don't lose Carolyn. You're afraid she won't come around anymore. And why would she? I wouldn't."

He pointed at Hulda. "I shoulda put a stop to this bullshit years ago. You've had too much control for too long and I'm takin' it back."

"You can't keep me here," Kimi said.

"You are a minor, girlie. I can lock you in your fuckin' room if I chose to and there ain't a damn thing you can do about it."

"If you lock her in her room, will you hire a housekeeper, cook, laundress, nursemaid and gardener to take care of this household?" Aunt Hulda demanded. "Because we both know *you* won't cook, or clean, or buy your own food, or even take care of your wife. You leave that responsibility to your children."

Her father glared at his wife. "I told you your sister would turn your daughters against us. Now do you believe me?"

Kimi looked at her mom. "You agreed to this?"

"He's my husband and your father. You're still a child, Kimberly—"

"I've never been a child! You didn't allow it! You expected too much from me." She tried to keep the petulance out of her voice, but this wasn't fair, and it wasn't right.

Aunt Hulda put her arm around Kimi and sent her brother-in-law a pitying look. Then she looked at her sister. "Listen to her, Clara. Eli is just upset that Carolyn married a man he didn't approve of. He's taking out his anger on your daughter. Are you going to let that happen?"

"Eli's decision is final, Hulda. I agree with him." She wheezed. "When you leave tomorrow, Kimberly won't be going with you."

Her stomach cramped. She felt the bile rise in her throat at the thought of being trapped here, in this house, for the next year until she could legally walk away.

"I'm sorry it's come to this, sister," Hulda said softly.

Kimi couldn't believe what she was hearing. Was the one woman she'd counted on giving up that easily? "Don't make me stay here," she pleaded. "I'll run away the first chance I get and no one will ever see me again."

"I know, sweetheart. But they're mistaken. They can't force you to stay here." Aunt Hulda glared at her sister. "In order to enroll your minor-aged daughters at St. Mary's, you gave the school guardianship over them. So technically, St. Mary's makes the final decision. And do you really think that they'll agree to terminate Kimi's education and their guardianship when neither of Kimi's parents has bothered to set foot at the school even *one time* in the six years she's been a student? No. I checked. And even if the school opts to remain out of the family issue, I can guarantee you I will *not* stand by and watch Kimi become an indentured servant."

"Feminist, hippie bullshit," her father grumbled. "A woman's job is to take care of her family."

"Then Mom failed at that pretty spectacularly, didn't she?" Kimi snapped.

"I have a parental consent form, signed by you, Clara, giving me guardianship on weekends, the summer and holidays," Aunt Hulda stated. "If you cared so much about her, then maybe you should've *read* the paperwork the school sent, rather than just signing it without reading through it. Although now, I am so very glad you didn't."

"You conniving witch," her mother said.

"I expected name calling from Eli, but not from my own sister." She patted Kimi on the shoulder. "I was afraid something like this would happen, so I already put your things in the trunk of my car."

"This ain't over," Eli warned.

"Yes, it is," Kimi said. "Now that I know neither of you have any power over me? I won't ever come back here. *Ever,*" she emphasized. She gave her mother, who'd started crying, a scathing look.

"Kimi, I'm sorry."

"Yes, you are. Goodbye, Clara." And because she was so upset, heartsick and disgusted, she looked at her Aunt Hulda and said, "Thank you for bein' the mother to me that she couldn't be. Now can we please go home?"

She walked out of the house and didn't look back.

Chapter Five

One year later...

Carson showed up at Cal's house an hour earlier than usual, so he knew something was wrong.

Cal poured his brother a cup of coffee and waited for him to speak, knowing even if he asked Carson what'd happened, he wouldn't talk until he was good and ready.

After a sip of coffee, Carson said, "Clara West died last night."

That surprised him, even when he'd known Clara wasn't in good health. "Sorry, man. How's Carolyn?"

"In shock mostly, even when we both knew this was comin'." Carson finally looked at Cal. "I fuckin' hate that I can't go along and support my wife without makin' it worse for her. The Wests don't want me there while they're deciding on final arrangements. It pisses me off that Eli will expect Caro to deal with everything because he's gotten used to it in the last year. And all of the years before it. If I don't go, I'll be worthless around here because I'll be worried about her. So I don't know what the hell to do, Cal."

Cal scrubbed his hands over his itchy face. He hadn't shaved in days. "You gotta go with her. If there's stuff they don't want you involved in, sit in the truck. But the bottom line is this ain't about them. It's about you bein' close by when your wife needs you. Because we both know she will need you. And the Wests don't got the right to keep you away from her."

Carson sighed. "Thanks for confirming what I already knew."

"Just needed to hear it from someone else?"

"Yeah." Carson stared into his coffee cup. "Caro asked me this morning how I got through Mom dyin'. I felt like a total shit because I didn't wanna tell her I don't remember much of that time, just the shock that she was gone. And the anger when Dad turned into a raging asshole because she'd died. And I sure as fuck can't tell her that I was mad at him because I didn't think he missed *her*—he just missed havin' a wife to cook for him and make his life easier."

Cal bit his tongue against asking whether Carson had said that shit to their grieving father. His twin had the subtlety of a jackhammer and zero tact. Carson ruffled feathers and left it up to Cal to smooth them.

"Dad learned to manage without Mom. Eli has been managing without Clara for long enough that caring for her father shouldn't fall on Caro's shoulders." Carson clenched his fist. "Goddammit, I won't let it. She's done more for her family than should be expected."

"That's what's bugging you. You're afraid you'll get thrown over for Eli West."

"The son of a bitch did it once, didn't he? Made Caro promise to look after her mother, while she was fuckin' *dyin'* and then made her also promise not tell anyone about it—including me, which caused problems between us."

"Whoa." Cal looked at his brother. "Run that by me one more time?"

"All that shit that went down after me'n Caro married? When I thought she regretted marryin' me 'cause she was at her folks' house all the time? That was because Clara was dyin'. She and Eli didn't want anyone to know. So my new bride was expected to keep the secret."

"Jesus, Carse. They didn't tell anyone?" Like Kimi? How mad would she be when she found out her sister and father had kept such a life-altering event from her?

"Harland knew since he and Eli are thick as thieves. Then after Clara went into the nursing home last month—"

"Did Carolyn keep that from her sister and brothers too?"

"About Clara bein' in a home? I'm not sure."

"Bullshit."

Carson's gaze turned shrewd. "Why're you getting pissed off?"

"Because Kimi and her brothers had a right to know about Clara's failing health. They would've had a chance to say goodbye."

"So what's worse, Cal? Carolyn tellin' her siblings their mother is damn near dead and none of them bothering to show up? Or Carolyn not tellin' them at all?"

"I don't fuckin' know, all right? I just understand how I'd feel if *you* made that big of a life or death decision without tellin' me nothin'."

Carson stood. "I get that. It's a fucked-up mess that's liable to get worse in the next few days. Hate to say it, but I won't be around much."

"I'll tell Dad what's goin' on."

"Thanks."

At the door, Cal said, "When you see Kimi, tell her if she needs anything I'm a phone call away."

That caught Carson's notice, as he'd known it would. "Something goin' on between you and Kimi I oughta know about?"

"We're friends. We spent some time together after your wedding." He wasn't about to try and explain the immediate pull between him and the blonde spitfire either, when he didn't understand it himself.

"You keep in touch with her the past year?"

Cal shook his head. He thought he'd see Kimi over Christmas break like they'd talked about last summer, but he knew from Carolyn that Kimi hadn't come home.

"I'll pass it along to her."

"Take care. You need anything else, holler."

"Will do."

Kimi stared at her mother's coffin as the priest droned on.

She sat at the far end of the pew in the second row between her brother Thomas and her Aunt Hulda. Her married siblings were in the front pew. Harland had parked himself right next to Dad.

She'd barely spoken to any of her siblings since she'd returned to Gillette three days ago. They'd had to postpone the funeral two additional days to allow time for Stuart and Thomas to travel back home.

Within an hour of arriving in Gillette, she'd been knee deep in boxes as she packed the few remaining items from her childhood. Her aunt agreed to store them indefinitely. Kimi hadn't offered to help sort her mother's things; she'd left that to Carolyn and her aunt. Most everything except for a few pieces of jewelry would be donated to the Catholic mission anyway. So as the two of them pawed through the few things that marked her mother's existence, Kimi had hid in the tall grass behind the shed and smoked. She'd rather get eaten alive by mosquitos and pick ticks off her skin than be in the same room with them, consumed by anger that the two people she loved more than anything in the world had betrayed her.

Aunt Hulda had known her sister was dying. That's why she'd taken a stand last summer, refusing to let Kimi remain with her parents. Dutiful Carolyn had known about their mother's failing health and she'd put her own life aside to care for their ailing mother.

Kimi couldn't find forgiveness for anyone for keeping that from her. She would—eventually—but not now, not until after she'd had time to process it all.

The priest spoke, pulling her out of her brooding. Then she knelt, crossed herself and listened to the choir sing another song about eternal love and redemption.

After that, everything was a blur. The trip to the cemetery. The repast in the church basement. She shook herself out of her reverie and reminded herself it'd only been thirteen months ago they were in this same place celebrating her sister's wedding.

The moment arrived. Carolyn and Aunt Hulda were surrounded by ladies from the auxiliary. Her dad and her brothers were holding court in the corner. She caught Carson's eye and he nodded.

No one paid attention to her when she hooked her purse over her forearm and headed upstairs.

Her brother-in-law was less than a minute behind her and he stopped her just outside the door. "Kimi. Sweetheart, I'm not convinced you're thinkin' straight. You sure you wanna do this?" Carson asked.

"I'm positive." She brushed past him and headed to the parking lot. After unlocking the trunk of her aunt's car, she waited while Carson unloaded the suitcases. He carried the big one, leaving the smaller one to her. Then she followed Carson to Cal's pickup, parked alongside the curb.

Her heart raced when she snuck a quick look at Cal. He wore his usual cowboy getup, jeans and a white shirt that stretched across his broad shoulders and chest. She couldn't see his eyes; the bright sunshine forced him to duck his head, keeping his face in shadow beneath his cream-colored cowboy hat. The muscles in his arms rippled as he hefted the enormous suitcase into the truck box.

Carson sidled in front of her. "After you've had some time to cool off, you call her and let her know where you are. Promise me."

"I will."

He offered her a brief hug, muttered something to Cal and then sauntered off.

Before Kimi uttered a peep, he effortlessly lifted her off her feet and wrapped her in his arms. "Sweet darlin'. I'm so sorry," he murmured in her hair.

She clung to him, breathed in the scents of sunshine and shaving cream and Cal. She felt normal for the first time in a week.

As much as she wanted to stay like that, they had to go before her family realized she wasn't in the church.

Cal set her down. Keeping her hand clasped in his, he towed her around the front of the truck and hoisted her into the driver's side.

She slid across the bench seat to her side.

He got in and popped the truck into gear. "You really want me to take you straight to the bus station? You have got a few hours until the next bus leaves, right?" He eyed her black dress and heels. "Do you really wanna sit in the dirty terminal in them pretty clothes?"

"Where else would I go?"

"Come to my place. I won't pester you to talk. You can sit out in the swing. I'll even feed you."

"The next bus leaves at eight tonight."

"I'll have you there in time."

It would be nice to just relax. "Okay."

Cal smiled. He picked up her hand and kissed her knuckles.

The day was oppressively hot. She rolled down the window and let the air eddy around her, her mind blessedly blank. For once she didn't mind the repetitive scenery.

"You really just plan on leavin' without a word?"

"I wrote Aunt Hulda a letter and taped it on the steering wheel of her car. She had more warning that I planned to leave because I'd given notice two weeks before Mom died that I'd be hopping a Greyhound at the end of the month. Carson has the letter I wrote to Carolyn." She'd kept both letters short.

"That's something, anyway."

Cal didn't speak again until they'd parked in front of his house. "You got anything in them suitcases that could melt? Gonna get hotter than sin out here."

"Makeup."

"It'd be best if I set your suitcases inside the house."

As soon as Kimi's feet hit the dirt, she heard yapping. She looked at Cal. "You have a dog?"

"Yeah. It gets lonelier livin' on your own than I imagined." A sheepish look crossed his face and she wanted to hug him. "She's good company. But watch out 'cause she's still a puppy."

"What kind of dog?"

"Australian shepherd-blue heeler mix." Cal lifted the luggage as if it weighed nothing. "She's in the backyard. You'd better change so she doesn't tear your stockings and dress to shreds."

Kimi snagged the small case and once they were inside, headed for the bathroom. She stopped in the living room. "You have furniture."

"Well, darlin', it has been over a year since you've been here. So why are you surprised?"

"I figured you'd be the type to leave it empty until you got married and let your wife decorate it."

"Nope. I can't go that long without a TV. And I have an aversion to a couch covered in flowers that I can't sit on."

In the bathroom she changed into a pair of floral pedal pushers and a sleeveless blouse, not bothering to put on shoes. Wandering through the house, she paused by the screen door to watch Cal playing with his dog. He'd ditched the western shirt in favor of his undershirt. Lord. The man looked even more muscled than the last time she'd seen him.

Then her attention was completely commandeered by a black and white and gray puppy bounding all over the place. The little dog would run toward Cal, stop, jump back, jump sideways. The puppy tore circles around him, yipping and barking until Cal was laughing so hard he had to rest on his knees. The puppy plopped right beside him, panting like crazy.

A warm, sweet feeling flowed through her at seeing such an unguarded moment. The instant she opened the screen door, the puppy's ears perked up. Then she emitted the cutest, most ferocious sounding barks as she raced forward to assess the threat to her master.

"Gigi!" Cal shouted. "Sit."

Gigi ignored him and jumped up on Kimi, her paws leaving muddy prints on Kimi's pants, her tail wagging crazily. "Hey, sweet girl." Kimi felt Cal's eyes on her. "You're a pretty little thing. Even your dog has those gorgeous blue eyes like yours." *Stupid thing to say, Kimi.* Trying to mask the awkward moment, she petted and praised the dog until the pup rolled over and showed her belly. She laughed.

"I'm happy to hear that sound," Cal said quietly.

"So you're not chastising me for laughing just a few hours after I buried my mother?"

"Not my business to judge you." He looked down at her hand on Gigi's belly. "She likes you."

"Puppies like everyone."

"True. But not everyone likes puppies."

"I love them. We weren't allowed to have pets, which I understand because they would've been neglected." *Just like I was.* "I swore that someday I'd have as many dogs as I wanted. Now I've added chickens to the list of future critters."

Cal crouched down. "Chickens? Why?"

"A friend of mine from St. Mary's was from an Ag family. I went home with her one weekend and found out that her mom raised chickens. I thought it was the funnest thing, gathering eggs in the morning. Who knew chickens had different personalities?

I went from knowing nothin' about them to wishing I had my own flock."

"Maybe someday you will."

"Maybe." Gigi whined and Kimi scratched under her chin. "Poor neglected pup. Are you hungry?"

"Speakin' of... Are you hungry?" Cal asked.

"No. But I wouldn't turn down a shot of Jack." Kimi kept ruffling the puppy's soft fur as she gazed at Cal. "You don't have to worry that I'm a minor. Two weeks ago I turned eighteen and I'm legally an adult."

A strange look flitted through Cal's eyes and then it was gone. "Look, I have no problem with you knocking back a shot. But I can't in good conscience give you booze and then put you on a bus with a bunch of strangers." He sighed. "Besides, I don't think you're thinkin' clearly. Grief screws you up."

She put her hand over the top of his as he pet the dog. "You're probably right. Still, I could use whiskey to take the edge off. But then I'd be shit outta luck as far as where to go because I won't spend another night under my dad's roof and I'm too mad at Carolyn to stay with her and Carson."

"Then have that drink and stay with me tonight. I've got plenty of room."

"Stay here with you?"

"Yeah. You could crash on the couch. It'd just be a friend helpin' out another friend."

Their eyes met.

Kimi saw nothing but sincerity in his steady gaze. Maybe the fact Cal hadn't heard from her or seen her in a year had cooled his feelings. "No girlfriend to get jealous?"

"Nope. Gigi here is my only girl."

"Okay. I'll stay. But you'll take me to the bus station tomorrow?"

"As soon as I finish chores I'll take you wherever you want to go."

"Thanks."

"Sit tight. I'll grab the bottle."

"The whole bottle?"

Cal smoothed a wayward curl behind her ear. "Somehow I don't think a single shot is gonna be enough for you."

Kimi played with the puppy until Gigi tired of fetch and settled in the grass. She crossed the yard and looked around.

In the last year Cal had added a roof over the cement slab, turning the area into a shaded patio. He even had two lounge chairs. He set two shot glasses on the stump that served as a table. Then he filled the glasses halfway before he sat next to her.

She picked up her purse, pulling out her cigarettes and matches. "Mind if I smoke?"

"Go ahead."

Cal passed over her shot.

It went down so smoothly she decided to have another.

After a bit, he said, "I know I told you I wouldn't pester you to talk, but I have to ask if you knew your mother was so sick?"

Kimi exhaled a stream of smoke and waggled her empty shot glass at him. "Can I answer that after I've had a few more of these?"

"It's your liver. But I'll warn ya. Have too many and you're on your own. I'm not the kinda guy who holds your hair back as you puke."

"I don't plan on puking."

His raised dark eyebrow was a blatant *we'll see.*

Following Kimi's second cigarette and third shot, Cal reached for her hand and threaded their fingers together. "Time to pay the piper and tell me what's goin' on."

That provided the push she needed to tell him everything. She didn't leave anything out, including what'd happened after she'd left his house last year.

"Hell, darlin'. That is some seriously fucked-up stuff."

"I know." She looked at him. "Carolyn didn't tell you any of this?"

He shook his head. "Carson only mentioned he'd known your mom was on death's door when he came over to tell me she'd died. And I ain't gonna lie. I gave him what-for about Carolyn keepin' you in the dark."

"Is that why you were so eager to help me?"

"Partially. And knowin' what happened after you left here that night explains a lot as to why I hadn't heard from you at all."

"I figured it was a one-night thing."

"Wrong. And you damn well know that's wrong."

Kimi stubbed out her cigarette, wondering how far she should go in this truth telling. "You're right. I'm sorry I didn't write you a letter or anything. I had some stuff to work out." As soon as she'd returned to Montana last year, she'd started making plans.

"It wasn't like I could ask Carolyn how you were doin'. Not even why you didn't come back for Christmas."

"She didn't know why I'd cut out all contact with Mom and Dad." She felt Cal studying her.

"So the last time you spoke to your folks...?"

"Was the night we had the big blow-up. So I've got a ton of guilt over that. But now I'm pissed that Carolyn didn't say shit to me about what was really goin' on with Mom. Neither did Aunt Hulda. So then I get here and find out every one of my siblings knew she was dying except for me." She firmed her wobbling chin. "How is that fair? The one child who needed to make amends didn't get the chance." That's when her voice broke and the tears started.

Cal picked her up and tucked her against his side. He whispered, "Hey. It's okay. Let it out, darlin'. I got you."

She blubbered in his arms until calmness and too many shots of Jack turned the lights out.

Chapter Six

Kimi slept like the dead.

Not that Cal would say that to her, beings she'd buried her mother today.

Gigi woke up wanting to play and brought the ball over. With Kimi sacked out almost on top of him, Cal kept one hand on her back and used his other hand to play fetch.

When the day began to dim, his stomach growled. He carefully shifted to standing and carried Kimi into the house, the puppy on his heels.

Cal paused in the living room, debating on whether to lay her on the couch. But if he wanted to watch TV, the noise would wake her, so he headed down the hallway to his bedroom. He started to lower her onto the bed when she stirred. Glancing into her face, a surge of tenderness overwhelmed him.

"So sleepy," she slurred.

"I know. Which is why I'm tuckin' you into bed, sweet darlin'." Cal left her clothes on and slipped her between his sheets. He sat on the edge of the bed, his heart heavy. He murmured, "Glad you decided to stay tonight."

"Me too." Kimi rolled over, giving him her back.

Gigi immediately jumped up and snuggled in beside her. "Good girl. Keep an eye on her."

Cal slept on the couch.

He tried not to disturb Kimi early the next morning as he rummaged in his closet for work clothes.

The bed squeaked and he turned around just as Kimi sat up.

At some point during the night she'd whipped off her shirt, leaving her in a black bra that emphasized the fullness of her breasts.

"Cal?"

Look at her face. But goddamn, that wasn't any better. She looked cute as hell, her hair sticking up all over the place. Her eyes slumberous.

"Hey."

She stretched her arms over her head and released a satisfied-sounding groan. "How long was I out?"

So much for not looking at her tits. "Twelve hours."

Kimi froze. "What? It's...morning?"

"Yeah. I've gotta check cattle but I'll be back around noon."

She looked at the other side of the bed. "Where did you sleep last night?"

"On the couch. Gigi stayed with you."

"So I took your bed and your dog." Realizing she was half-naked, she pulled the sheet up. "I'm sorry to be such a pain in the ass, Cal."

"You had a rough day. You obviously needed to sleep. I'm just glad you were here and not on a bus to god knows where."

"Vancouver."

"What?"

"You've said 'on a bus to god knows where' a couple of times. I'm goin' to Vancouver and then I'll get on a boat that's takin' workers to Juneau."

Stunned, he said, "You're movin' to Alaska? Why?"

Kimi tossed her hair over her shoulder. "One of my classmates was from Alaska. She kept talkin' about how beautiful it was, and how much better the wages were up there. She said she could get me a job workin' in her uncle's dry cleaning business. At first I thought she was just blowing smoke, but it turned out she was serious. Right before we graduated, I got an official letter from the business offering me the job. They're paying my travel expenses to Juneau, but I have to sign a one-year contract." She yawned. "It's too great of a chance to pass up."

"Did you tell your family?"

"I told Aunt Hulda because she had to find a seamstress to replace me, but I didn't tell her too far ahead of time because she'd try and talk me out of it. I let Carolyn know in the letter I left her. And I don't give a damn about the rest of my family."

"When do you start?"

"Whenever I get there. I had to call them long distance to tell them my mother died and I'd be delayed."

He wanted to be supportive, but Alaska? Christ. "Well, that's... great they're so understanding."

"Cal. That wasn't even close to sincere."

"It just threw me, okay? That's a long way from here, especially for someone—"

"Who's never been south of Denver or north of Miles City?" She leaned forward. "That's exactly why I *have* to go. I thought you, of all people, would understand."

"My travel experiences are as limited as yours have been, so darlin', I'd be lyin' if I said I understood. But I'm damn proud of you for doin' something adventurous. Few people have the guts to do it." That'd sounded somewhat supportive.

"But?"

"But if you don't have a set schedule to meet, and you need a few days to sort things out, you can stay here."

That took her aback. "Thanks. I'll think about it."

"Make yourself at home and we'll talk when I get back, okay?"

She nodded. "Can Gigi stay with me?"

"'Fraid not. I'm trainin' her. Consistency is important."

"I understand." Kimi met his gaze head-on. "Please don't let Carson know I'm still here."

"I won't." He closed the door behind him.

For the next several hours, Cal kept his mind off Kimi. Luckily he was working with Charlie so he didn't have to lie to his twin—not that it'd work since Carson could always tell when something was up and Cal rarely saw the need to lie.

He returned home a little after noon. He tracked Kimi down in the backyard, where she was tearing the far flower bed apart. Weeds were flying over her head. She looked like a blonde tornado.

The pup bounded up to her, licking her until Kimi laughed. "All right, all right. I'll pet you. Let me take the gloves off."

Cal couldn't help but return Kimi's grin. "She'll probably get you dirty since she's been runnin' through the muck all mornin'." He knew it was stupid to be jealous of the way she petted and cooed at his dog.

"She's sweet. I'd like to steal you, Gigi girl."

"I imagine a dog ain't welcome on a cross-country bus."

Her hand stopped mid-pet and she blurted out, "Were you serious?"

"About?"

"About letting me stay here a few days if I needed to."

His pulse raced and he fought to stay calm. "Yeah, I was serious."

"Good. Because these flowerbeds have been sorely neglected and are in need of tending."

So am I, sweetheart.

Christ, he sounded like a needy pussy.

He refrained from asking if the sad state of his flowerbeds was the only reason she'd decided to stick around. "I'd welcome your help. Only thing I've done since you were here last year was fix the irrigation system."

"You should've cleaned out the deadfall." She pushed to her feet. "Are you hungry?"

"Starved."

"I made you a couple of sandwiches."

"You did?"

"Don't get your hopes up that it's as good as what Carolyn makes."

"Lord, woman. I'd never compare you. So get that outta your head right now. I'm just happy there's food that I don't gotta cook myself."

Kimi stopped in front of him. "You left so fast this morning that I didn't get a chance to say thanks for...everything yesterday."

Cal curled his hand around the side of her face, using his thumb to wipe a smudge of dirt from her cheek. "You don't have to thank me."

"Because that's what *friends* do, right?"

Fuck that. Enough of this politeness. This awkwardness.

He slid his hand around the back of her neck. "That's what we are? Friends? Because to be honest, darlin', I don't wanna be your friend."

"What do you want to be?"

"This." He lowered his head and took her mouth in a commanding kiss.

She fisted her hand in his shirt, pulling him closer.

God. He hadn't imagined this passion. He hadn't forgotten the heady taste of her. His cock went rock hard. His common sense took a hike.

And Kimi kissing him back with equal ferocity just fueled the fire that'd been on a slow burn for far too long.

He wanted to clamp his hands on her ass, wrap her legs around his hips and carry her straight into his bedroom.

She ripped her mouth free and jumped back. "Ouch!"

"What?"

"Gigi bit me!"

Cal glanced down at his dog, who barked happily as if she'd done a good thing. "Gigi!" He crouched down and wrapped his hand around her nose, forcing her to look at him. "Bad. No bitin'."

The dog cowered, whimpered and peed. But she got the point that he was the alpha.

"Lay. Down," he said tersely.

Gigi dropped to the grass and tried to bury her nose in it, away from him and his reprimands.

Cal slid his hand up the inside of Kimi's calf. "Show me where she got you. Wait. I see it." A raised white mark circled by red.

He ran his thumb across it and Kimi snapped, "Don't. It hurts."

"That's because Gigi didn't bite you. Something stung you and the stingers still in there."

"Oh. That'd explain why it burns." She looked at Gigi. "Sorry I doubted you, girl."

Gigi's tail thumped.

"Hold on to my shoulder. I'm gonna scrape it off with my fingernail." He pinched the skin and then ran his nail down the bump, knocking the stinger out. "Done. I'll doctor you up to keep it from swelling. Hang on."

She gasped when he picked her up and headed for the house. "You're such a show-off, McKay."

"What?" He whistled for Gigi.

"Proving that you can pick me up and carry me around whenever you please."

"I don't see you tryin' to get away."

"I'm not stupid."

"That means you like bein' carted around?"

"By you? Yes. You are just so...big and strong." She squeezed his biceps. "Are you all hard muscles everywhere?"

Cal waggled his eyebrows. "If we'da kept kissin' like that? One muscle in particular would've gotten really hard."

Kimi blushed. But she smiled—a strange mix of sly and shy. "Damn bees. Butting in when you were about to give me my very first hands-on demonstration of the birds and the bees."

Surprisingly, he didn't miss a step when understood what she was saying. "So all of them boys in Montana are idiots for not tryin' to get with you?"

"They were boys. I didn't trust they knew what to do." She buried her lips in his neck and gooseflesh erupted. "But you're all man and you know *exactly* what to do."

"Sweet Jesus, Kimi."

"You'd rather I pretended to act shy?"

"Hell no. I don't know what you want from me."

"That's the thing, Cal, you *do* know. I just wanted you to understand that I want it too."

Inside the kitchen, he set her on the table.

When she looked at him with that expectant gaze, he fastened his mouth to hers again for a very thorough kiss. "Don't move," he said against her lips.

Cal washed his hands and mixed a paste out of baking soda and water. Then he took a knife and spread it over the area. "That should take the sting out. Let it dry and don't pick at it."

"Thanks." She pointed to the fridge. "Don't forget about your sandwiches."

Damn. He'd been so hungry for her that he'd forgotten about actual food. He washed his hands again and opened the fridge to find two sandwiches wrapped in wax paper. She'd speared a dill pickle with a toothpick and stuck it on top. Why that amused him, he didn't know. "Is that pierced pickle a warning to me?"

Her eyes widened. "No! I was trying to make it look like a fancy deli sandwich."

"I appreciate the thought. But I'm a simple guy." He held up the plate. "You want one?"

"I already ate."

"More for me." When Cal sat at the small table, Kimi started swinging her legs back and forth. "Darlin'. Relax."

"Okay."

That lasted about thirty seconds and two bites of his ham and cheese sandwich before she was back at it.

"Kimi. Why can't you sit still?"

"Because bein' this close to you makes me want to jump out of my skin."

At that point he didn't have a prayer of keeping his hands off her. "Same goes." He placed his palm on her left thigh and stroked the outside of her knee with his thumb. He tried to pretend he was calmly eating his sandwich, but the warm softness of her skin, and the sweet and earthy scent of her made him hungrier for so much more than just food.

Her chest rose and fell rapidly. She'd start to shake her foot, only to stop immediately.

"This isn't workin'. You need to put that leg up anyway. So why don't you go lie down while I finish eating."

"Where?"

Cal locked his gaze to hers. "The couch. Or my bed. Your choice."

Chapter Seven

She bit her lip and he had to sink his teeth into his sandwich so he wouldn't be tempted to bite on that lip himself. Then she slid off the table and moved to the sink to wash her hands and face.

He eyeballed her ass and those shapely legs, wondering what was going through her mind.

But she exited the kitchen without saying a word or looking at him.

Don't listen for the direction of her footsteps.

Gigi whined and he glanced over at her, sitting by the cupboard where he kept her food. "I know, girl. Gimme a sec, okay?" He tossed her a piece of crust and started on the second sandwich.

After he finished, he filled Gigi's food and water dish and set it on the patio. He washed his hands and face. Rinsed his mouth out. Counted to twenty and went looking for her.

Cal paused in the doorway to the living room. The cushions on the couch were still askew from him tossing and turning last night, but Kimi wasn't there.

Hot damn.

First thing he saw when he passed through the doorway of his bedroom were the bottoms of her small feet. Then his gaze traveled up her legs and holy fuck, her ass cheeks peeked out from her black panties. His eyes followed the length of her spine past the band of her bra—yep, she'd ditched her shirt too—and stopped at the smooth curve of her shoulder.

Kimi had propped her head on her hand, sending her blonde curls spilling across her other shoulder. Her eyes were wide. Her lips parted. Her breathing uneven.

"Fuckin' hell, woman. You're half-nekkid."

"You're upset about that?" Her gaze dropped to the fly of his jeans. "'Cause I'm gonna call bullshit on that, cowboy, seeing's as you've got a lie detector in your pants."

"Oh, I'm really goddamn far from upset. I'm closer to speechless if you wanna know the truth." He scrubbed his hand over his face, unable to tear his eyes away from the bounty spread out before him.

"I like that look in your eyes, Cal."

"What look is that, darlin'?"

"That you're really happy I'm not sixteen anymore," she teased.

He smiled, knew it bordered on wicked and didn't care. He started toward her.

"Why aren't you askin' me why?"

"Why what?"

"Why now? Why you?"

"Because I *know* why."

That seemed to confuse her. "You do?"

"Uh-huh." Cal kept his eyes on her as he removed his boots. "One, we've had this lust thing goin' from the first time we met. Two, you'd like to escape from the sadness in your soul for a little while. Three, deep down you know it'd piss your dad off if he found out his youngest daughter let a McKay pop her cherry. Four, I'm here, I'm experienced and you trust me."

Kimi cocked her head at him.

"Am I wrong?"

"No. Actually you hit my thoughts dead on. Except you left off reason number five."

"Which is what?"

Her gaze started at his sock clad feet and roamed north, until their eyes locked. "You are the best lookin' man I've ever met. Your muscular body makes my mouth go dry and my panties wet."

Lust and need for her didn't roll over him; they hit him like a coal train.

"You're sure this is what you want?" he half-growled.

"Very sure. Very, very sure," she repeated.

Cal started to lower onto the bed, but Kimi held her hand up. "If I'm half nekkid, it's only fair that you are too."

The pearl-snap buttons made shedding his shirt easy. He grabbed a fistful of his tee and yanked it over his head. Kimi's eyes widened as she got her first look at his bare chest. Then her avid gaze followed the movement of his fingers as he popped the button on his jeans and tugged down the zipper.

His Wranglers hit the floor, leaving him in his boxers and socks.

"Did you get all that—" she gestured to his body, "—just from doin' cow stuff?"

Cow stuff. "Yeah, darlin'. Doin' cow stuff keeps me buff." He grinned. "Now lay on your belly so that paste on your calf has time to dry."

"What will you be doin'?"

Cal leaned over and nipped her ass, and grinned when she expelled a gasp. "How about you can the questions and let me be in charge."

"Okay." She paused. "But I do have one last question."

Of course she did. "What?"

"Why did I like it so much just now when you bit me on the butt?"

He let his breath ghost across her skin as he moved up her body. "That's what I'm gonna find out. What you like." He started out by kissing her shoulders and the back of her neck. He rested on his haunches and mapped every beautiful inch of her back and arms. "Then I'm gonna show you what I like." He slipped his hands around her waist, marveling that he could almost span it with his hands. Then he trailed his fingers up and down the back of her legs. He didn't touch the bottoms of her feet—she squirmed enough when he kissed her anklebones. When he kissed the curve of her ass cheeks, he got his first whiff of her arousal and it ignited his senses like a drug.

After he unhooked her bra, he said, "Turn over, darlin'."

Kimi kept her eyes closed after she'd rolled over. Her breathing was ragged. Her skin had flushed the prettiest color of pink.

"Look at me when I'm touchin' you."

"Why?"

"Because I said so, and last time I checked, I was in charge."

Her eyes flew open.

He grinned. "I figured that'd get your attention."

"I've never done any of this."

"I know." He traced her collarbone. "Which is why I want you to see, hear, feel, taste and smell everything that we're doin'."

"Smell?"

Cal buried his face in the side of her throat. "Yes, smell. Right now your skin is giving off a scent that's drivin' me out of my fuckin' mind." He nuzzled the start of her hairline. "And I know you like the way I'm touchin' you..." He rubbed his lips over her ear. "Because I can smell how wet you are between your thighs."

She tried to cover her face with her hands.

He chuckled. "Nope. Never be ashamed of the way your body reacts. It's the sexiest thing in the world to know that I can make your pussy wet, make your nipples hard, make you sweat and beg for more."

"When you put it like that..." She flattened her palms on his pecs, sifting her fingers through the dark hair covering his chest. "Show me more, Cal. Show me everything."

"Get rid of the bra because it's keepin' me from putting my mouth on you."

She tossed aside the bra so fast he felt the strap hit the bottom of his chin.

Cal felt a growl starting when he got his first look at her naked tits. Christ. They were so full and round and topped with cherry red nipples that his mouth just homed in on them.

The connection of his mouth to her nipple sent her back into a hard arch.

So he did it again on the other side.

That time Kimi released a soft groan.

He sucked softly. Then he swirled his tongue just around the tips as he cupped the heavy warm weight of her. Cal explored and filed away Kimi's reactions. But she loved everything, teasing licks, hard suction, the soft-lipped bites and even the scrape of his teeth.

As he started to kiss his way down her smooth belly, he felt her body tightening up. "You want me to stop?"

"No. I don't know what I'm doin'. I feel like I'm laying here like a lump while you're doin' everything."

Cal rubbed his lips over the fine blonde hairs below her belly button. "You'll get your turn. Right now, I want you to reach down and pull your panties off."

Kimi slid her hands down her sides and slipped her fingers beneath the lace at her hips. She could only reach as far as her knees, and Cal took over from there.

When she was fully naked, he rested on his knees at the end of bed and just looked at her.

"What?" she demanded.

"You are very well put together, Miss Kimi. I'm just admiring the sight of you in my bed with your eyes and body wanting me like this." Keeping his eyes on hers, he traced her slit with his knuckle, from the top of her mound to her opening. He did it twice more and watched her squirm. "Do you touch yourself?"

She blushed. "There weren't a whole lot of things to do at Catholic school in the evenings."

"So you had your hand beneath the blankets diddling yourself every night?" Why that image turned him on really made him feel perverted. Especially when he imagined her wearing that Catholic schoolgirl outfit while she did it.

"After my roommate went to sleep. Or when I was alone. But it wasn't every night."

He placed his hands on the insides of her knees and pushed her thighs open, then slid his hands up to frame her pussy. "You know what I'm gonna do?"

She shook her head.

"I'm gonna put my mouth right here—" he rubbed his thumb side to side over her clit, "—and here—" he dragged his thumb to the opening to her body, "—and in here." As he said *in here* he gently pushed his thumb inside her.

Fuck she was tight. And wet. His brain just took over and screamed *gimme what's mine*. He bent his head and licked straight up her slit.

"Oh. That's—"

"Christ, woman," was all he rasped out before he dove in, fastening his mouth to her pussy lips, sucking at her warm flesh, while his tongue delved deeper, searching for a complete taste of her.

"I like that."

"Then you're really gonna like this." He focused all his attention on her clit. Sucking. Licking. Teasing. Absolutely going to town on her like he'd wanted from the first time he'd seen her.

It wasn't long before she released a soft wail and she came apart.

Feeling her twisting and writhing against his face with such abandon had him growling as he tongued her relentlessly. The rhythmic pulses slowed but he didn't give up his prize until she slumped against the pillows with a soft, "Holy shit."

Grinning, he forced himself to back off, letting her catch her breath and her balance. He nuzzled the insides of her thighs, and the skin between her hipbones. He nibbled on the outer curve of her hip as his hand snaked up to play with her tempting tits.

Kimi trailed her fingertips up and down his forearm. "I want to get my hands on these impressive muscles. So is it my turn now?"

"Nope. It's still my turn." Cal settled himself between her thighs.

She stiffened up. "Wait. What are you doin'?"

"Havin' another go at you."

"You don't have to."

"Are you kiddin' me? I want to. Trust me; I could stay right here all fuckin' day." He peppered kisses over her mound. "So sexy watchin' you come undone."

"But what about you?"

He looked up at her. "Makin' sure you're wet and ready *is* for me, 'cause I don't wanna hurt you." He didn't have a monster cock, but even if she hadn't been a virgin, he'd take extra care with her because she was a tiny thing.

She curled her hand around the side of his face. "Thank you. I'm glad I waited for you."

"I'm glad you waited too," he murmured against her hip. "If I do something you don't like, let me know."

"I don't think that's possible."

Cal raised his eyebrow. "We done talkin'? 'Cause I got a better use for my mouth."

She blushed again.

This buildup was purposely slower. He stretched her with one finger, then two, licking her delicately everywhere but directly on her clit. Once he knew she could take direct contact, he still kept his suction soft.

When her hands moved from clutching the sheets to clutching his head, he knew she was close. So was he. If he didn't get inside her soon, he'd spill all over the goddamn sheets.

"Yes. Stay like that. I'm..." She gasped when she started to come.

Her clit pulsed beneath his flickering tongue and her pussy muscles squeezed his fingers.

He glanced up and saw those hard nipples and the sheen of sweat across her chest. Gooseflesh rippled across her abdomen and the muscles in her legs twitched. Cal wanted to roar, throw himself on top of her and pound into her until she screamed his name.

In the aftermath, Kimi's pussy got wetter. Hotter. And he knew it was time.

Cal eased his fingers out and started to back away, but she murmured, "Not yet."

That's it, sweetheart. Tell me what you need.

"What?"

She absentmindedly petted his head. "It feels different when you use your fingers."

"Feels good?" he asked, pressing soft smooches to the curve of her mound.

"Yeah." Kimi pushed up on her elbows, her eyes half-lidded and a smile curving her lips. "Is real sex better than that?"

"Darlin', that *was* real sex."

"You know what I mean."

Cal crawled up her body, looming above her on his hands and knees. "I'll let you judge for yourself." He kissed her neck. The sweep of her collarbone. The ball of her shoulder. He nuzzled the tops of her breasts. "I want you. But I need to know that you're you ready. Because I'm still at the point where I can stop."

"But I don't want you to stop."

He pushed back and stood. He dropped his boxers and waited, letting her look at his cock.

"Does it hurt when it gets hard like that?"

What a question. "Nope."

Kimi sat up and crawled to the end of the bed, her lithe body as sexy and slinky as a jungle cat. "It's a lot...redder than I thought."

"I thought you were gonna say it's a lot bigger than you thought."

"That too." She looked up at him when she was close enough that he felt her breath teasing the tip of his dick. "Is it weird I wanna know what it feels like to have that in my mouth?"

"Such a curious kitty-cat," he murmured. "But no, it ain't weird. It's hot as fuckin' fire."

"Can I?" she asked right before she enclosed the head between her lips.

"Ah, fuckin' hell, woman."

"What did I do wrong?"

"Nothin', it just surprised me."

She swirled her tongue around the head, then pushed back so she could wrap her fingers around the base. "You weren't kiddin' about it bein' hard." She feathered her thumb across the middle of his shaft. "But it's soft too."

Cal had to put a stop to this. Especially when her hair fell forward, teasing the tip as she experimented with sliding her closed fist up and down as she licked him. "Kimi. Stop."

When she looked up at him with those big blue eyes, he curled a shaking hand around her face. "Let's leave your turn at touchin' me for later."

"Okay. I just wanna do it all."

"We will. One thing at a time." He swept his thumb across her lips. "Right now gimme that mouth." He urged her upright onto her knees and lowered his head. He kissed her, running his hands down her tangled hair and over her chest, until his neck screamed in protest. Then in a smooth move he couldn't repeat again if he tried, he brought them both down to the mattress with her on top.

Kimi lifted her head, breaking the kiss. She slid her chest down and then back up. And down again. "That feels good."

Every downward glide had her ass connecting with his cock. Cal clamped his hands on her round cheeks and opened his mouth on her neck.

She trembled above him.

He rolled them again and rested on his elbows above her. Her mouth opened so hungrily as she kissed him, her hands were all over him as if she couldn't decide where to touch him first. So he gently pinned her arms above her head. "Leave 'em there. Spread your legs and make room for me." When he lowered his full weight onto her, she arched up, letting her head fall to the side and fully exposing that gorgeous neck. "You ready for this?" he murmured.

She thrashed when he started a slight rocking motion against her. "Yes. Please. Show me."

The knuckles of his hand got wet with her juices when he reached between their bodies. "Look at me."

Their gazes connected. Then their mouths.

He pushed the head of his cock in and stopped. An odd thought crossed his mind and he smiled.

"What's so funny?"

"Just thinkin' about that joke 'just let me put the tip in, if you don't like it I'll pull out'."

"This is a serious moment, Cal. How dare you crack jokes?"

He lifted his head to look into her eyes.

She smiled at him. "I like the tip, so keep goin'."

Cal eased in and swallowed her surprised gasp when he filled her hot, tight little cunt completely.

Fuck. That felt fucking amazing.

Breathe.

Don't rut on her.

Kimi shifted and slipped her arms around his lower back, smoothing her hands over his ass.

He kissed a path to her ear. "What's that tight squeeze on my ass supposed to mean, former virgin?"

"That I'm taking my turn at touching you."

"Bossy former virgin," he muttered.

"I'm fine, Cal. You're holding back. I'm ready."

But he wasn't. Her pussy clasped his shaft so tightly he'd probably only last ten strokes before he'd blow. "Wrap those sexy legs around my waist," he murmured in her ear.

The change in position opened her up a little more and she buried her face in his neck.

Cal pulled out, paused, and slid back in. "Feels so damn good."

"For me too, so don't stop."

He didn't stop, but he kept the rhythm slow and steady. Letting his chest rub on hers after hearing her practically purr the first time he did it.

And yet, somehow, the awkwardness remained.

Getting the first time out of the way was tempting. He could show her how much better it was the second time, and every time after that.

So he changed tactics and stopped with the sweet, sweet lovin' and started to fuck her.

All the awkwardness disappeared and Kimi got into it.

Really into it. Moving underneath him, kissing his chest, biting his ear all the while that tight pussy squeezed him.

"Cal," she breathed against his throat, "it's happening again."

"Don't tense up, darlin', just let it happen." He nudged her face until she let her head fall back. He latched onto the sweet spot on her neck and sank his teeth in. In hindsight Cal hadn't the foggiest on why he'd done that, but it worked.

Kimi gasped and thrashed, her hips driving upward, searching for that perfect amount of pressure until she found it.

She cried out his name. Her fingernails dug into his ass hard enough to leave gouges. Her pussy went tighter yet, so his cock felt as if he'd stuck it into a vacuum as it sucked out every bit of seed.

He came harder than he'd ever come before.

He came so hard that when he remembered he was still on earth, not in the damn stratosphere, Kimi was soothing him. Kissing his neck. Pressing her fingertips into his lower back. Murmuring sexy sweet nothings into his ear.

When Cal opened his eyes, Kimi looked at him with awe. Then she kissed him.

Not an ordinary kiss, but one that filled him with hope, and a sense of purpose.

This woman belonged to him. She was his purpose. She needed him in a way no one else did. And he sure as hell needed her.

So it sliced him to the quick when he understood in order to have her forever, he'd have to let her go for a little while.

"Cal?"

He had no idea how long he'd been lost in bliss. He glanced down at her. "You are so damn pretty." He kissed the corner of her jaw. "I'm thinkin' I could chain you to my bed and just tell everyone you left. That way I could have you to myself."

"Selfish, are you?"

"When it comes to you? Yep. Without apology." Cal shifted slightly and she sucked in a sharp breath. "Sorry. I'll move. Just hang on." He pulled out as slowly as he could, studying her face for signs of pain.

She blinked at him and whispered, "I can still feel you inside me."

"I suspect that'll be the case for several more hours." He bussed her forehead. "Stay put." Then he scooted off the bed and headed to the bathroom. As he soaked the washcloth in cold water, he splashed water on his face.

A bout of nerves came over Cal and he returned to the bedroom. He hesitated by the side of the bed. Come to think of it...he'd never been with a virgin. Was he supposed to clean his seed off her and then hold the cool cloth between her legs as they cuddled under the covers and talked about what'd happened?

As he debated with himself, Kimi sat up and held out her hand. "Stop bein' weird and get over here."

He was so crazy about this woman. She just seemed to look at him and know what he was thinking. He relaxed and got back under the sheets.

Kimi rolled onto her belly and propped her head on his chest. He pushed her hair off her damp cheek. "What?"

Her gaze continued to roam over his face. "A great lookin' man like you shouldn't even notice someone like me. But here I am. In bed naked with you."

"Or...an old timer like me shouldn't catch the notice of a hot young thing like you."

"Why do you always counter everything I say?" she demanded.

"Because darlin', it riles you up and I love it when you get feisty." Cal pulled up the sheets and tucked her along his side. "You plum wore me out. Let's take a catnap and when we wake up I'll answer all those question swimming in your eyes."

"Okay. But I'm pretty sure I'd rather have a hands-on demonstration on some of the...more explicit questions I've got."

"That, I can do. As many times as you want."

Chapter Eight

On day five of Kimi's stay, Cal had been very thorough waking Kimi up. So thorough that he hadn't realized he'd missed meeting Carson until he heard the crunch of tires on gravel through the open bedroom window.

He glanced at the clock. How the fuck could it be seven-thirty?

Shit. "Carson is here."

Cal didn't need his brother barging in and seeing Kimi's things spread all over his house. He kissed Kimi and hopped off the bed, quickly jamming his legs into his jeans, foregoing his boxers. He yanked a T-shirt over his head and didn't bother putting on socks or boots.

Kimi watched him, a satisfied smile on her sleepy face.

"Stay in here."

"Even if Carson is your brother, it is impolite to show up at someone's house at seven-thirty in the morning, Cal."

"Seven-thirty is practically noon for ranchers and I was supposed to meet Carse an hour ago. And I'm never late, so he knows something is up."

Gigi started barking like crazy. "Come on, girl."

Cal closed the bedroom door behind him. Good thing Kimi had been adamant they lock the doors at night or Carson would've just walked in.

Gigi whined and raced toward Carson immediately after Cal opened the front door.

Carson crouched down to pet the pup. "Looks like *you're* ready to move cattle, dog, which is more than I can say for him." Carson gave Cal a once-over from his bare feet to his uncombed hair. "You sick or something?"

"Nah. I just stayed up too late and overslept. It happens."

"It never happens to you." Carson rolled upright. "I don't imagine you were out tearin' it up because you don't reek like booze or look hung over. So I'm bettin' your late night has something to do with that hickey on your neck."

He shouldn't love it so much when Kimi sucked and bit on him, but Jesus it got him so fucking hot he'd rather deal with shit than ever ask her to back off. "You caught me."

Carson jerked his chin toward Cal's bedroom. "She's still here, ain't she?"

"Yeah. So if you'll give me a little time to get ready, I'll meet you at Dad's so we can get this underway."

"You ain't gonna introduce me to her?" Carson paused and gave Cal a big grin. "That's because I know her, don't I?"

"Don't be a jackass," he said with an edge.

It was the edge that tipped Carson off because normally Cal was even-keeled.

"So how long you need to get ready? I don't see a car here so you've gotta run her home first?"

Fuck. He hadn't thought of that. "Nope. She said she's fine sticking around today."

"Is this why you've been distracted the past couple days?"

"I haven't been distracted," Cal scoffed.

"Yeah, you have. Even Charlie mentioned it yesterday."

"So I screwed up one goddamned thing. Like Charlie has room to talk. He's been distracted the last *year*."

"Charlie thought I'd be preoccupied this week with all the shit that's been goin' on with the Wests. He volunteered to pick up the slack if I had to leave, which is why he mentioned it. He just didn't think he'd have to be picking up your slack too."

"I told you I'd do my part and you're relyin' on Charlie? That's fuckin' perfect, Carse. Next you'll tell me that Casper's watchin' me too."

Carson crossed his arms over his chest. "Even that shouldn't worry you if you've got nothin' to hide, Cal."

Gigi barked and scratched at the door to go back inside.

"What's with her?"

Cal ignored the question. "I'll meet you at Dad's in twenty, okay?"

"No can do. Tell me what's goin' on. You're never this secretive."

"I ain't allowed to have secrets?" he snapped. "That's bullshit. You've got your life with Carolyn which is separate from us workin' together. I respect that. You need to learn to do the same for me."

"Who is this woman who's got you all twisted up in knots?"

The door opened behind him.

Kimi stepped onto the porch. "It's me."

Cal had never seen Carson so shocked. Under different circumstances his bugged-out eyes would've been funny as hell. Snagging Kimi's wrist, Cal tugged her against the side of his body.

After his gaze winged between them, Carson said, "You've *got* to be fuckin' kiddin' me. You've been here since Cal picked you up?"

"Yes."

"And you two are what? A couple now? You're livin' together?"

Cal held his breath. He wasn't sure what would fly out of Kimi's mouth.

"What's goin' on with me'n Cal isn't any of your business, Carson. I will say that he's letting me stay here as I sort some stuff out."

"That whole tale you spun in that letter to Caro about movin' to Alaska was a lie?"

Kimi shook her head. "I'm still goin'. I just didn't leave the day of the funeral."

"When your sister finds out—"

"You *will* keep your mouth shut, McKay," Kimi snapped, getting right up in Carson's face. "Carolyn is to know nothing of this. You hear me? *Nothing.* My letter explained everything. She knows she won't hear from me for at least a month. And I'm sure she's got plenty of other shit to deal with and doesn't need anything else piled on top of it. So just go about your business and let me'n Cal sort this out on our own time frame."

Straight to the point. Kimi was a lot like him in that respect, so Cal didn't feel the need to add anything else.

"But I fuckin' hate keepin' a secret this goddamn big from my wife. She finds out, who's she gonna be pissed at? Me."

"The only way she'll ever find out is if you tell her," Kimi shot back at Carson. "Promise me you'll keep your mouth shut."

Carson looked at Cal.

Cal pulled Kimi back and wrapped his arms around her as they faced his angry twin together. "I don't ask for much, but I am askin' you to respect mine and Kimi's wishes on this, Carse."

"Fine." He stepped back. "Don't bother showin' up at Dad's today to work. He'll know something is up between us because I'll probably spend the whole day pissed as hell." He stormed to his truck.

Fuck that. "Explain to me why *you're* pissed as hell," Cal demanded.

Before he climbed in, Carson spun back around. "Because if Carolyn knew about the two of you bein' involved? She'd be beyond happy. And my woman could use a dose of happiness this week. But I can't even give her that."

Cal kept Kimi close as Carson's truck burned gravel down the road.

Neither of them spoke for a while.

Finally Kimi said, "Is this gonna cause problems between you two?"

"I won't let it. Carson wants to give your sister the world. He knows there wouldn't be anything on earth better for her than havin' you with me, livin' up the road from them."

"I agree. But his concern is for you too. He probably thinks I'm just toying with you and I'll leave you broken-hearted."

He knew Kimi wasn't toying with him, but the jury was still out on what her leaving would do to him. Not that she'd given him any indication of when she planned to go. "That's why it's better we keep this between us. No need to get her—or anyone else's—hopes up for something that ain't gonna happen." At least not for a while.

Kimi spun into his arms. "I know we said we'd take this day by day. But the longer I stay with you, Cal, the harder it's gonna be to go."

"I know that, darlin'. For me too." He framed her face in his hands. "So you've gotta pick a day and stick to it."

Her eyes clouded and she bit her lip. "The day after tomorrow."

"Let's make every moment count." Cal settled his mouth over hers and kissed the daylights out of her. "Now that I've got the day off, let's celebrate."

"Doin' what?"

"What do you think?" He scooped her into his arms.

She laughed. But her laughter died when she noticed he wasn't headed in the direction of the bedroom. "Uh, Cal? Where are we goin'?"

"Outside."

"Ooh, kinky. We gonna do it in the swing?"

"No, we're gonna finish weeding the back section and then when it gets too hot we'll spend the afternoon in the cool, dark bedroom, doin' all sorts of kinky things at least until suppertime."

"Gotta love a man with a plan."

Being with Cal had been the best week of Kimi's life.

Not only was he sweet, thoughtful, slyly funny and just so easy to be around, he made her body sing. And the bonus was the man was a horny devil; he made love to her morning, noon and night. Literally.

He had the most inventive ways to wake her up—his cock rubbing against her clit as he feasted on her tits and came on her belly. Hiking her hips in the air and eating her from behind, then slamming into her like a pile driver. Spooning in behind her, those skillful fingers manipulating her clit as he rocked in and out of her. But she'd woken up before him yesterday morning, taking his soft, sleeping penis into her mouth until it hardened. Then she sucked him off and wouldn't let him touch her.

But Cal had made her pay at lunchtime. First he'd used piggin' string to tie her arms together and tied them to the headboard. He'd swatted her ass hard while he whispered dirty talk to her that'd made her wet because she wasn't expecting that from the laidback cowboy. The crazy man had made her come three times—once with his mouth, once with his fingers and once with his cock—and then he'd gone back to work with a smug smile on his face.

Last night when he came home, he'd been quieter than usual. After the sun went down, they sat side by side on the swing and she'd finally bugged him into telling her what was wrong.

"I was rough with you earlier. Rough and kinky and Christ, up until a few days ago, you were a damn virgin. It's obvious that when I look at you, I just goddamn want you any way I can get you, and I forget about the fact you're eighteen."

That had pissed her off. She climbed on his lap and covered his mouth with her hand.

"I oughta spank *you*, Calvin McKay, for talkin' such crap. Am I some mealy-mouthed maiden who can't speak up for herself? Hell no. There are two people in bed doin' what we've been doin' and if one of us wanted to stop, then one of us is smart enough to say so. Have I said no?"

He shook his head.

"Have you said no?"

Another shake of his head.

"And I'm also smart enough to figure out that you haven't asked the other women you've been with to do the fun, kinky things we've been doin'. Or maybe you thought that as a sheltered Catholic virgin I wouldn't *know* what's considered normal when it comes to sex, so you decided you'd sneak in some kinkier stuff to see if I balked."

His eyes narrowed.

"Which probably would've been true...*if* I hadn't found my Aunt Hulda's erotic how-to books. She had a whole box of them. I have no idea where she got them, but I think because she was a nun who married a priest, neither of them knew shit about sex and they had to learn it from books."

He mumbled something beneath her hand.

"So you *don't* get to act sorry. Because I'm not. Not. At. Fucking. All. I liked that you don't treat me like every other woman you've bounced on or like I'm some fragile doll you can break. I like that you play rough with me. If you woulda gone too far, I'da told you."

And he'd proved how sorry he was for bringing it up. Twice.

So things were going good. So good that she mentioned to him she'd considered not going to Alaska.

But because Cal was smart, in addition to being loving and thoughtful, he was refusing to let her stay.

Refusing. To prove he wasn't joking, he'd tossed her suitcases on the bed half an hour ago and reminded her of the bus schedule in Spearfish.

Kimi brooded as she sorted and repacked everything she owned.

The silence between them was deafening.

Then Cal's strong arms encircled her. She closed her eyes and let the warmth and comfort of his sheltering body envelope her.

"I'm crazy about you, Kimi West. You know that."

She slumped against him. "I know."

"You may act older than you are, but it doesn't change the fact that you *are* just eighteen. You have adventures ahead of you." He kissed the top of her head. "I want that for you. To have the excitement of doin' something new. You deserve a chance to see who you are away from your schooling and your family. You've been plannin' this a long time—longer than you've been with me—and I'd never ask you to give that up."

Even if I want you to ask me to stay?

Rather than phrase her response nicely, she felt her anger and fear of the unknown get the better of her. "Oh, so now that you've had me in your bed for a week, you're tired of me? You're gonna show me firsthand the McKay reputation for fucking until you get your fill and then moving on?"

"You don't have to leave in anger," he said softly. "You already left your family that way, don't lump me in with them. There's no need to say hurtful, untrue shit just because you can." He brushed his mouth across her ear. "You think this is easy for me? You think my selfish side ain't screamin' up and down that I'm a fuckin' idiot for makin' you go? It'd be a damn sight easier askin' you to stay. We both know that. But I never wanna see them pretty blue eyes glaring at me with resentment. I never wanna see a far-off look on your face that tells me you're wondering how different your life would've been if you'd taken that chance. That's a big goddamn burden for me to bear, sweetheart."

"But how is making me go any different than what my family did by making my decisions for me?"

"Because *you* made this decision on your own. I'm just makin' sure you stick with it."

Tears welled up. "Why are you bein' so reasonable?"

"One of us has to be." He kissed the hollow below her ear. "Finish up and get those suitcases off the bed, woman, so I can strip you bare and give you something hot and hard to remember me."

At least he hadn't said he wanted to make love to her one last time.

So it was sort of ironic that's how it played out. Cal touching her everywhere with those skilled hands. Knowing exactly how to make her purr, moan and scream. Him kissing her from the arch of her foot to the crown of her head and everywhere in between.

He dragged out the pleasure. When they'd both reached the point of no return, he whispered, "Come with me. I wanna hear you say my name."

"Cal."

"Look at me."

She met his gaze and shattered beneath his pounding thrusts.

When the throbbing ebbed, she saw something deeper in his eyes and it soothed her ragged edges, knowing he'd be as messed up by her leaving as she was. Knowing their time together had meant as much to him as it had to her.

They remained locked together as their sweating bodies cooled and their heartbeats returned to normal.

After a few deep kisses, Cal slowly rolled off her. He snatched his clothes and left her to get dressed.

Kimi gave the rumpled bed one last look before she lugged her suitcases into the hall. Then she wandered through the house and out the back door.

She cried during her goodbye to Gigi. Maybe if she got the tears out of her system now, she wouldn't sob as she watched Cal's taillights fading off into the distance. The pup licked away her tears and whined. "Be a good girl. He'll need extra doggie snuggles, so stick close." She ruffled the soft fur. "But feel free to bite any other women he brings around."

Gigi yipped agreement.

She shouldered her purse and saw her suitcases were gone. She found Cal leaning against the driver's side of his pickup, squinting at something across the horizon.

"What?"

"It feels like rain. God knows we need it."

"So we're talkin' about the weather now?"

Cal smirked. "Darlin', sixty percent of rancher's conversations are about weather and thirty-nine percent of conversations are about cattle."

"And the other one percent?"

"Everything else."

Kimi slid her hands up his chest. "Glad to know I made the one percent for a little while."

"You've been ninety-nine percent this week and you know it." He tugged her against him. "I've been wrestlin' with how to say this, or if I oughta say it at all. I know you have to go. But when you get tired of the gypsy life, come back here. Come back to me. I'll be waitin' for you. For however long it takes."

She lost the ability to breathe.

"I trust in this, what we have between us, to know that it'll last. I'm confident enough to let you go, because I realize this ain't the right time for us, but there *will* be a right time. And you will be back."

"So you'll just...?"

"Live my life as I've been. I'm not askin' for any promises. I don't need them because I know in my soul that you're mine." Cal tipped her head up and gazed into her eyes. "You've been mine, Kimi West, since the moment I saw you. My heart knew it; it just took a year for my head to catch up."

"And for me to grow up."

"Well, that was hangin' over us too. But now..." He kissed her, almost chastely, but that kiss was a promise. "Now I'm stakin' my claim on you. And I'll be right here, waitin' until you're ready to do the same to me."

Then Cal stepped aside and opened the driver's side door for her.

The drive to Gillette was silent. But after Cal's declaration there wasn't anything else to say anyway.

Cal unloaded her bags and sat with her in the terminal after she'd bought her ticket.

When the intercom announced boarding, he walked outside with her.

The exhaust fumes from the bus eddied around them, churning the stiflingly hot air until she felt she was choking and couldn't breathe.

"Take care of yourself, darlin'."

"I will."

"Have fun, be safe. Shoot first, ask questions later."

She laughed through her tears.

"Keep in touch. Let me know when you get settled."

"I'll miss you." *I already miss you.*

He kissed her forehead.

"Cal—"

"Go," he said gruffly, "before I change my goddamned mind and make you stay."

She stood on tiptoe and kissed his chin, his dimple, and those beautiful lips. She whispered, "See you around, cowboy," and forced herself to get on that bus. She took a window seat on the opposite side of where Cal had stood.

But when the bus pulled out, ten minutes later, she saw him, standing there, watching her leave.

Later that night Cal sat on the tailgate of his truck, throwing the ball for Gigi, trying like hell to focus on the sunset, or all the shit he had to catch up on starting tomorrow. He tried to think about anything besides the hole in his gut that half a bottle of whiskey hadn't filled.

The sun had dropped below the horizon. He rested back on his elbows, wondering if he oughta sleep out beneath the stars tonight. He knew his bed smelled like her and that might just do him in.

A truck barreled up the driveway at breakneck speed. He wondered if there'd ever come a day when his brother didn't drive like a damn idiot.

Carson jumped out of the truck and Gigi was right there, her ball in her mouth, her tail wagging happily. He tossed the ball a few times before he grabbed a brown paper bag out of his truck and ambled over.

Cal kept his gaze on the horizon. A bottle of Wild Turkey appeared in his peripheral vision.

"I figured you might need this," Carson offered as an explanation.

"Why? That stuff tastes like shit."

"You're gonna drink until you pass out so you might as well not waste the good stuff. And this shit ain't half bad comin' back up in the middle of the night."

"Thanks for that. I thought maybe you were just cheap."

"There's that too." Carson cracked the top and took a long pull. He couldn't withhold a shudder. Then he passed the bottle to Cal.

He swallowed a mouthful and almost spit it out. It went down the wrong pipe and he ended up coughing like he'd just taken his first drink.

His brother pounded him on the back. Then Carson did the oddest thing; he left his hand there in the middle of Cal's back. A moment passed and he stated, "She left today."

"Yep."

Carson squeezed his shoulder and let his hand drop. "I hate that for you."

"I hate it for me too." He swigged from the bottle. "She wanted to stay."

"She did?"

"Yeah." He knocked back another drink. "I made her go."

"Shit. Why'd you do that?"

"She needs to experience things I can't give her."

"Did you get that lame-brained idea from a dime-store card or something?"

"Fuck you."

Carson laughed. "I ain't gonna pretend to understand why you did that."

"As I was sittin' here, alone with my dog, drinkin' myself into a stupor, I don't understand why I did it either." He paused. "I miss her, Carse. I had one week with her and I shouldn't miss her this goddamned bad but I do."

"Length of time don't mean shit, Cal. You know that from seein' how fast Carolyn became everything to me."

"Yeah, well, I was hopin' to avoid that emotional shit."

His brother laughed again. "And you stepped right in it—with a West girl to boot."

Cal said nothing. He just drank.

So did Carson. Finally after a bit he said, "This ain't no passin' thing with Kimi, is it?"

"Nope."

"She knows that?"

"Yep."

"Then she'll come back."

"You sound so sure."

"And you aren't?"

"I was." Cal sighed. "I mean, I am. It's the waitin' that's gonna suck. Even when I know she's worth the wait."

Carson clapped him on the back. "Good thing we've got plenty of ranch matters to take your mind off it for the next couple of years."

"Thanks for that."

"Anytime." He jumped off the tailgate. "You gonna be okay tonight?"

No. "Yep. But I'll probably be hung over tomorrow." Cal pointed at the Wild Turkey. "And I'm blaming it on you."

"You've done your share of mornin' after whiskey therapy with me so it's only fair I return the favor."

Chapter Nine

Year one...

Kimi doll,

I can't tell you how big my smile is when I see a letter from you in my mailbox. Folks driving by probably thought I'd won the sweepstakes.

I was glad to hear you found a different place to live after you left Juneau. The landlord sounded like a real piece of work. While I understand Alaska is the last frontier, it can't be comfortable sleeping with a gun under your pillow every night. A beautiful woman like you is bound to attract attention, so *be* _careful_.

Not much has changed around here. Working cattle, getting ready for market. Carson and Carolyn are so crazy about Cord. He's a cute little bugger. Total chip off the old block. My dad seems happy to have a grandson. Even if he is half West. I guess your dad is acting happy about it, even if Cord is half McKay. Although your brother Harland ain't happy that Carolyn birthed the first grandchild. Carse has mentioned Eli stopping by their place a time or two. I wish you were around to keep Carolyn company. I know she misses you. If the signs I'm seeing in nature are correct, I suspect it'll be a hard winter. Yep, you knew I'd get to talking about the weather at some point. I wonder how your sister will fare being cooped up in a trailer out in the middle of nowhere all day with a baby.

I did some improvements around the place, not a lot of other things to do. I tilled up the flower beds in the far back corner the past three weekends. After watching nothing come up in the last two years, I figure I'd start over with the planting next spring. So if you've got advice on what to plant, and where, I'm all ears.

Gigi got with puppies again. I had a devil of a time giving away the last batch. Although, I don't know if I told you that your brother Darren took a male pup. Guess he's working out well as a sheep dog. But I'll probably buck up and get her spayed after this litter.

As always I've been thinking about you. Hoping you're finding what you need up there in the frozen tundra.

I'm not going anywhere, sweetheart. You know where to find me.

Cal

Year two...

Calvin sugar britches,

You always start with an endearment so I thought I'd follow suit with something new.

I know you're busy birthing calves and other assorted cow stuff. Carolyn says Carson drops into bed exhausted every night so I'll bet your nights are even shorter, since my brother-in-law has a wife, and a kid, and you, being the standup guy, probably tell him to go home and you'll handle it. I hope you're taking care of yourself and eating more than peanut butter and jelly sandwiches. Not that my food choices are any better up here—it's heavy on elk, caribou and salmon. I tried moose. It was the most god-awful stuff I've ever tasted. Besides bear. I actually barfed it was so nasty.

Speaking of bears...someone had to kill a bear right in the middle of town last week—Fairbanks does seem like the last frontier sometimes! Locals say that once a bear gets a taste for people food, they won't go back into the wild. Then they become violent when they're denied food, so there's no choice but to put them down. I've been careful when I hike to take a gun with me. But with my luck, I'd probably shoot myself.

I realized when I read back through all the letters you've sent me, that I never gave you specifics on what to plant, so I've drawn up a detailed garden plat. It's not to scale, but it'll give you an idea of what goes where, and the ideal distance between the rows and clumps. The time to order seeds is <u>now</u>. I know you're getting the same seed catalogue I am since I signed you up for it, so I've made notes on which seeds you oughta buy.

My job is all right. At least working in the laundry department keeps me warm during the day. The winters up here are brutal with the limited sunlight, but like I told you before, the summers make it worthwhile. I've saved up enough money that I can travel to Kotzebue on the coast this year for a whole month. I'm going whale watching, and out on a commercial fishing boat for a week. A friend of mine who did the boat trip last year said they got close enough to Russia to see the coastline and some military ships. So if you don't hear from me, don't tell my sister I might be in a Russian prison for trespassing! Just kidding. But since I'm taking off during tourist season, I'll probably lose my job. I'm ready to move on anyway. I don't know where I'll end up—that's the fun part.

It's hard to believe I've lived here for two years. Sometimes it feels like I've never lived anywhere else. And other times, I miss the dusty wind and sagebrush in Wyoming.

I definitely miss you.

XOXO
Kimi

Year three...

Kimi,

Sorry I haven't written much lately. The days and nights have dragged on in recent months and I've been hibernating. Carson says I've been grumpy as an old bear, but most days I feel like a snapping turtle that people poke with a stick just to see how long it'll take me to snap.

When I'm not refereeing my brothers and our dad, I work on projects around the house and out in the barn. Stuff that I hope to show you one day soon. Very soon.

I miss you. I thought you being gone would be hard. But not this hard.

Been forever since I've seen your pretty face. Do you look different? Do you feel different? With the way you move around, I can't help but think that you're restless. I can't help but hope that maybe you've had enough of moose country and you're ready to head back here.

I told you I wouldn't pressure you. I'm trying not to, but I'd give everything I own to hold you in my arms right now.

Take care of yourself. But sweetheart, I sure wish it was _me_ taking care of you.

Cal

Year four...

Cal,

I was so happy to see in your last letter that you were able to take some time off and go to Colorado Springs. I always wanted to ride the train to the top of Pike's Peak. I imagine the view was something. But I've gotta say—we've got bigger mountains here in Alaska.

I found it...interesting that you didn't tell me who you traveled to Colorado with.

With sunlight until almost midnight, the growing season here means I've seen some huge pumpkins. There are dahlias the size of dinner plates. If I could, I'd get a job working outside. At least in the summer.

You asked if I went out and whooped it up now that I'm living in the big city of Anchorage. Nope, because I don't have any free time. But yes, I still have time to be your pen pal. Aunt Hulda sends me long letters about the funny and stupid things she does when she doesn't have me to watch after her. I know it's her way of telling me she misses me. Carolyn hardly ever writes me. It seems weird that she has two boys now and I've never seen either one of them.

I know it seems like I move around a lot. But it's what I want after being stuck in one place so long. I've seen so many incredible things and I know there's so much more I haven't seen. I wish you were here to share it with me.

Behave yourself, cowboy.

Kimi

Year four...

Kimi,

Been a while since I've heard from you. Your sister doesn't say much about what you've been up to, so that makes me think that maybe you found yourself a mountain man. I'd worry you'd been eaten by a bear or were lost at sea, but Carolyn did let it slip that you were way far north now in Prudhoe Bay. So being at the North Pole I figured maybe you were working for Santa Claus.

I just keep on, keepin' on. Dad is buying land left and right and it's taking a toll on me'n Carson because it seems like we can never catch up. It's been a lot of driving and that gives me way too much time to think about your last few letters and how you talk nonstop about how great it is in Alaska. I worry that you're not ever coming back here.

I need to hear from you. It's hard not knowing if you've moved on with someone else.

Cal

Year five...

Calvin McKay, you jackass,

I haven't MOVED ON WITH SOMEONE ELSE! Although the accusation makes me wonder if I might've been better off if I had.

~~I can't believe you~~

Okay, I had to take a break and have a smoke. During the little time I can stand to spend outside in this frigid air, in the damn dark, I realized Carolyn couldn't tell you what happened because I haven't told her. She worries too much and the woman has enough to worry about these days.

First of all, I moved to Prudhoe Bay from Anchorage when oil was discovered up here. I was lucky enough to get in on the first wave of workers, which means we got a tiny house with two bedrooms for four women—sadly that's more than the shacks most people are living in. I've been working in a bar/restaurant 70 hours a week. It is crazy up here. The ratio of men to women is like 200 to 1. There's not enough housing, food is more expensive here than in New York City, vehicles have to run 24 hours a day or they'll freeze up, and there's no sun at all from November to mid-January. So it's dark, crowded, and cold as a witch's tit in a brass bra. There's rumors of a new pipeline that's gonna be built straight down the center of the state, which means more guys moving up here hoping to strike it rich. The money is out of this world. That's the only reason I'm staying. But I ain't gonna lie. I don't know how much longer I'll stick around.

Just to clear things up, you haven't heard from me because there was a screw up with the mail. I swear the Pony Express had better service! I found out <u>nothing</u> got transferred to my new address in Prudhoe Bay from my old address in Anchorage for the last eight months. So I didn't even get this letter, and the three others you sent before that, until last week. So I understand why you think I was avoiding you. I wasn't. And when I hadn't heard from you, I thought maybe you were done with <u>me</u>. But I didn't have the guts to ask my sister if you were seeing someone. Oh, and I wasn't screwing around with Santa's elves either, and I'm sure you're making a crack about how I'm short enough that I'd fit right in with them.

What happened to you saying that you'll wait for me? And your claim that we are meant to be together? I oughta come down there and kick your butt for having so little faith in me, Cal.

Kimi

Two weeks later...

Kimberly Jo,

A little bitty thing like you kicking my butt? Not gonna happen, sweetheart.

But you're welcome to try.

Cal

One week later...

Cal,

I don't wanna fight with you. I miss you too much.

XOXOXOXOXOXOXOXOXOXOXOXOXO

Kimi

Five days later...a wire via Western Union...

Kimi looked at the message from Cal.

<u>COME HOME NOW</u>

Well, he couldn't have made it any clearer than that.

And it was clear enough to her that it was time to go home.

Chapter Ten

It'd taken Kimi a month to get everything settled in Alaska and return to Wyoming.

She hadn't told her sister or any of her family she was coming back.

Not even Cal knew. She wanted to surprise him.

Her stomach had butterflies from the time she'd left Seattle heading east on I-90 until the moment she pulled into Sundance.

She'd never been great with directions, but she managed to find his house, even in the dark.

But there wasn't a light on and his truck wasn't in the drive.

Disappointment flooded her that he wasn't home.

On a whim, she drove by Carolyn and Carson's trailer. Her gut clenched at seeing her mom's car sitting there, as well as a pickup. The absence of another pickup meant Cal wasn't here either.

As much as Kimi wanted to knock on the door and meet her nephews, and see her sister for the first time in years, she didn't pull in. There'd be time for a reunion after she'd reunited with Cal. They might not come up for air for days.

She drove back into Sundance to look for a place to eat.

During her slow perusal of the four blocks that made up the main drag, she counted two bars and two restaurants. Both the restaurants were closed. Maybe one of the bars served food.

She parked in the middle of town and walked to the first bar, The Golden Boot. But loud, bad country western music blared from inside and it looked like there was a cover charge to get in.

Skip that one.

The next bar was The Silver Spur. It looked equally busy. After spending the last year working in a bar, the last place she expected to find herself on a Saturday night was in a smoky honky-tonk. She hoped the cowboys' manners were better than the roughnecks' she was used to dealing with.

Kimi ducked into the bathroom first. She took a moment to check her makeup. After living in the backwoods and dressing for warmth and comfort—in that order—she feared she looked like a lumberjack. She peeled off the flannel shirt and shoved it in her purse. That left her in a sleeveless T-shirt. At least it was low cut so she didn't look like a guy.

She removed the band from her hair and fluffed it up. It fell nearly to the middle of her back. Most days she just pulled it back into a ponytail to be done with it.

As she applied another coat of mascara, she wondered if Cal would recognize her. With the longer hair and more angular lines to her face and neck. Hard physical work had melted the baby fat off her.

Two women burst into the bathroom, laughing and drunkenly holding on to one another.

Kimi washed her hands and would've tuned out their high-pitched chattering, but one word stopped her cold.

Cal.

"Who's Cal here with?" the blonde asked with confusion as she puckered her lips in the mirror.

"Oh. I don't know. Seems like he's with a different one every weekend."

She didn't consider that it might be some other guy named Cal. She knew it was him.

If that jerk was rotating girls every weekend after he'd sent her the edict a month ago...she'd gut him just like she threatened to do to his brother.

After exiting the bathroom, she started her search for him down the farthest side of the bar. Her pulse pounded in her neck and her ears, giving her a slightly buzzed effect that sharpened her senses. Or maybe she was delirious from hunger.

A guy grabbed her elbow and said "Hey, sugar, you lookin' for someone? 'Cause I can be anyone you want."

His drunken friends laughed.

Kimi smiled at him. "Yes, actually. I'm lookin' for Calvin McKay."

Another guy butted in. "Afraid you're too late, little bit. He's already made his choice tonight."

"Sure wish I could cherry pick 'em like he does," another man grumbled. "Seems all he's gotta do is say his name and the ladies spread their legs."

The first guy elbowed him. "Don't be crude."

"I appreciate your help, but is Cal still in here?"

"Yep. In the middle booth." The guy looked at her suspiciously. "You ain't from around here. What'd you want with him?"

"I've gotta give him something."

"What?"

"A knuckle sandwich," she said sweetly.

Kimi threw her shoulders back and weaved around the bar. After she stepped around a group of women, she had a clear shot of him.

Her heart leapt, her stomach flipped and her breath caught. The man was such a stunner. That midnight black hair. Those captivating blue eyes. The slight curve to his lips. That square jawline. That damn dimple in his chin. He wore a black cowboy hat and a white shirt that set him miles above the rest of the guys in this place. When he lifted his beer bottle and drank, she shamelessly watched the muscles in his throat move as he swallowed. She remembered the feel of those muscles beneath her lips. The taste of his skin in that spot. His fingers tapped his beer bottle with agitation—a nervous tic she hadn't seen before. Her thoughts rolled back to how those thick, rough-skinned fingers felt trailing over her body. Then Cal smiled at something the person across from him said, and Kimi went hot all over.

Mostly under the collar.

Tempting to buy a drink so she could toss it in his face. But she'd handle this the mature way.

Kimi knew the instant Cal noticed her. He squinted as if he might be seeing things. Then he froze. She slowed down her walk, enjoying every moment of his confusion.

The anger that flared in his eyes surprised her. He lowered his beer to the table.

She managed to keep the quiver out of her voice when she said, "You didn't really mean *come home now*, did you?"

Without taking his eyes off of Kimi, he said, "Move," to the woman sitting beside him.

"Are you always this rude?" she complained.

"Get out of the booth, right fuckin' now," he snarled at her.

Kimi couldn't move even if she'd wanted to.

But the woman realized Cal wasn't kidding and scrambled away from him.

Cal slid across the bench seat as quickly and efficiently as a predator stalking prey. He loomed over her, his gaze locked to hers. He lifted his hand to her face. The instant his fingers touched her skin he growled. "About goddamned time, woman." Then he captured her mouth in a kiss that started out sweetly exploring, but became desperate.

Everything faded but the heat of Cal's body, the hunger in his touch and in his kiss. Kimi clung to him, feeding his desire with her own.

Finally when someone yelled, "Take it outside, McKay," they broke the kiss. But they didn't move very far apart.

Cal clutched her hand tightly. "Come home with me."

"What about your date?"

He frowned. "What date?"

"The woman sitting next to you."

"She's a friend of my brother Charlie. She just plopped herself down and I don't even remember her name."

"Good. Because I was getting ready to launch myself into a hair-pulling fight for you."

Cal traced the line of her jaw with the backs of his fingers. "While the thought of you in a girl fight over me turns me on, there's no need to get into a titty slappin' match to prove anything. You own me."

She kissed the dimple in his chin. "Prove it."

He draped his arm over her shoulder and steered her through the crowd and out the door.

In the middle of the parking lot, he stopped and pulled her against him, clamping one hand on her ass and the other around her jaw. "Why didn't you tell me you were comin'?"

"I wanted to surprise you."

"Did you really think after I sent you the wire demanding you get back here that I'd be out with another woman?"

She twisted her head out of his hold. "You *were* sitting with a woman, Cal."

"I explained her."

That was all the explanation he gave—and all she really needed.

"We're leavin'." Then Cal grabbed her hand and led her across the parking lot almost at a run. Her shorter legs had a hard time keeping up with his longer strides. But the man was on a mission and he didn't stop until he reached his pickup.

He pushed her against it and kissed her like she was everything in the world he needed to survive. When he finally released her mouth, they were both breathing hard. Kimi was surprised they weren't already naked.

"Get in the truck or I'm going to fuck you right here, in the parking lot, Kimi. Where anyone can see just what you do to me." He nuzzled her ear. "And how goddamn much I missed you."

"That sounds like a threat, cowboy."

"No, sweet darlin' mine. It's a promise."

Kimi loved that Cal was so forthright in what he wanted. She knew the instant he put those big hands on her, she'd be putty. So she needed to remind him that she could make him weak-kneed too. "Cal."

"God, you smell so good." He kissed the hollow below her ear. "I didn't change the sheets on my bed for a solid month after you left until they lost the scent of you. Of us."

His sweet talking—how she'd missed it.

"Over the past five years, I started a list of the things I'd do to you when I saw you again." Cal's lips teased hers with barely there kisses. "For the longest time the top fantasy was your legs spread, that hot pussy bared to me as you sat on the tailgate of my truck." He moved his lips across her jawline to her other ear. "I'd be on my knees, eating my fill of your wet cunt, feeling your sweet little clit pulsing beneath my tongue as I made you come again. And again. And again."

Kimi trembled when his hot breath drifted across her neck.

"The goddamn taste of you," he growled, "was so vivid in my mind that just thinkin' about swallowing your sweet juices made my cock so fuckin' hard that I shot my load without even touchin' myself." He rested his forehead in the crook of her neck. "That's what you do to me."

If she liked his sweet talking, then she flat-out loved the way the man dirty talked. Her head was awash in the sexy images he'd painted, but this one time, she wanted to lead the charge instead of following his. She turned her head until her lips connected with his ear. "If you're tryin' to get me hot and bothered, Cal McKay, it's workin'. But I've been that way since the moment I saw you tonight."

"Jesus. Can we stop talkin' and start doin'?"

She laughed. "I had my own list of what I wanted to do to you when I saw you again."

"Yeah?"

"Oh yeah." She blew in his ear and smiled when he shuddered. "Wanna know my top fantasy?"

"You're killin' me here."

Kimi reached down and undid his belt buckle. "I'd rather show you." She dropped to her knees and scraped her fingernails down his erection as she unzipped his jeans. After she yanked the tight denim down his muscular thighs, she slid her hand into the opening of his boxers and pulled out his cock.

"Brace your hands on the truck, Cal."

He hissed out a breath and said, "Fuck, woman," but he did what she asked.

The man wasn't an idiot.

She didn't see a reason to tease him—this time. She craved his surrender and she needed to know if the passion between them was as overwhelming as she'd remembered.

The moment she pulled his rigid shaft into her mouth, all the way to the root, Cal's taste and scent consumed her. That's all it took. She knew she hadn't imagined the explosive need. She wanted to give him everything of herself and to be everything that he needed.

Curling her hands around the backs of his thighs, she drove his cock in and out of her mouth. Sucking hard. Using her teeth and tongue. Losing herself in the heady taste of him. Working him over unleashed something primitive inside her. Her world became the wet sucking sounds of her mouth. The hard throb of her nipples that matched the tightening pulse between her thighs. She reveled in his harsh grunts. The rocks digging into her knees. The firm muscles of his thighs clenching beneath her hands.

Every bob of her head, every deep stroke when his cock hit the back of her throat, she silently chanted, *you are mine, Calvin McKay. Mine.*

One of Cal's hands dropped to her head and he grabbed a fistful of hair. "Kimi. Please."

She hadn't been holding back, but that gruff plea...god. She almost came from his admission of need.

Tightening her lips and speeding up with shorter strokes sent him sailing over the edge immediately. Hot, thick, salty bursts of his seed saturated her tongue and she swallowed greedily.

Cal loosened his grip on her hair. He absentmindedly stroked her face as he tried to level his ragged breathing.

Kimi slowly eased back, letting his semi-hard cock slip from her mouth. As she stood, she kissed her way up his body, over his clothes. She paused for a moment, letting her cheek rest against his thundering heart.

They remained like that for several moments. Not because it was awkward, but because they both needed the connection.

Then Cal forced her head back and took her mouth in a blistering kiss. By the time he finished proving to her that the reins were firmly back in his control, she could hardly breathe.

"Understand one thing," he said directly into her ear as he pulled his jeans up.

"What?"

His belt buckle jangled when he refastened it. The noise was strangely sexy in the silence between them. "It's not gonna be sweet, sweet lovemaking the first time." He sank his teeth into her earlobe, sending a delicious spark of pain through her. "I'm gonna fuck you hard. *Hard*," he repeated, just in case she'd misunderstood.

"You think I'm gonna say no?"

His deep chuckle against her neck vibrated straight to her clit. "I think you'd better get in the damn truck."

"I'll follow you."

Then Cal was right in her face, those blue eyes flashing impatience. "Kimi. After five years I don't think I can be away from you for five goddamned minutes. We'll come back for your car tomorrow."

"Cal. Everything I own is in my car. And after waiting five years for me, the drive to your place will pass in a heartbeat, won't it?"

He rested his forehead to hers. "I don't think my heart was beating at all until the moment I saw you again."

Lord. She promised herself she wouldn't cry. Not right away. "I can't handle sweet right now with you. Give me rough. Give me hard."

A slow, devious grin spread across his handsome face. He smacked her butt hard enough that she yelped. "Sweet darlin' mine, I can do rough. And I already warned you that's it's gonna be hard. So with that in mind...you've got ten minutes to have this sweet little ass parked in my driveway. I'll be waitin'."

Chapter Eleven

When Kimi woke up naked the next morning, sore in all the right places, she wasn't surprised to see Cal's side of the bed was empty. But since Gigi slept at the foot of the bed, hopefully that meant Cal hadn't left to do ranch chores yet.

Her things were still in her car so she grabbed Cal's T-shirt off the dresser and slipped it on.

The scent of coffee lingered in the hallway. She heard voices and shot a quick glance at the living room as she passed by, wondering if Cal was watching the news, but the room was empty with the drapes drawn.

In the kitchen, she saw him leaning against the back wall talking on the phone. Even in a relaxed posture—shirtless, barefoot, his hair mussed, scruff on his face—he was something. Sexy, commanding.

Hers.

Last night had he *ever* shown her that he belonged to her as much as she belonged to him. The passion between them was unsurpassed.

He glanced over at her. A beautiful light sparked in his eyes. "Carse. I gotta go." As he listened to whatever his brother said, his hungry gaze took her in from head to toe. "I'll let her know. Uh-huh. Yeah, me too. Thanks." He hung up the phone and untwisted the cord before he started toward her.

"Morning, lover," she cooed.

"You're wearin' my shirt."

"All my clothes are still in my car and I have no idea what happened to what I wore last night since you stripped it off me before we were even in the house." She tilted her head back to look at him when he loomed over her. "Good lord. Are our clothes hangin' off the porch railing where anyone who drives by can see them?"

"Don't care." Cal kissed her with more than just a good-morning peck. Guess he didn't care that she hadn't brushed her teeth. He kissed her with such surety, yet she was surprised by how his big body trembled.

Kimi wreathed her arms around his neck, offering him support, letting him know she was as affected by this as he was.

When he finally ended the kiss, he buried his lips in her hair. "I've wanted you here since before you stepped foot on that bus. Now that you *are* here...I'll do everything under the sun to make sure you stay. Not for just a week, Kimi."

Forever hung between them, but for once, the word didn't scare her. "So what's goin' on today? Don't you have cow stuff to do?"

She felt him smile against the top of her head. "Carson said he'd take care of it. I'm to bring you over to see Caro and meet the boys ASAP."

"First, I need coffee. Then clothes."

"Pour yourself a cup. I'll get your bags." Cal stepped back. "I'm putting your things in my bedroom. You got a problem with that?"

"Nope." She considered how fast her response had been as she reached up for a cup. Staying with Cal as a visitor for a week when she was eighteen and had nowhere else to turn had been one thing; living with him indefinitely and having everyone in the community knowing it was another. And with the way he'd kissed her in the middle of the bar last night? Hell, her brothers had probably heard about it.

She slammed a cup of coffee like she was knocking back a shot. She turned around and saw Cal hadn't left the kitchen. He was right there, leaning against the doorframe, beefy arms crossed over his chest and a big grin on his face. "What?"

"Damn. I never knew you wearin' my T-shirt would distract me so much. Go on and reach for another coffee mug. Or better yet…bend over and check the floor, I think I might've dropped something down there."

"Such a funny man." She smirked. "Maybe later."

"I don't suppose I could talk you into comin' outside in that so I can show you some stuff?"

"Right now? Cal. I don't have on any underwear!"

"It ain't like anyone besides me is gonna see you." Without waiting for her answer, he scooped her into his arms and started toward the front door.

"Where we goin'?"

"You'll see."

"You like carting me around, don't you?"

"No, I fucking love it."

It had been dark when she'd pulled up last night, and she had other things on her mind besides checking out the buildings. But now she could see all the improvements Cal had made out here.

He'd painted the barn and put a new roof on it. He'd repaired the corral and several horses were at the trough drinking. Before it'd just been broken down and not useable as a penning area. "That looks good. You keep your horses here now?"

"Yeah. Mine and Carson's most days. We've been bringing the heifers here to calve. I like getting out of my bed and just walkin' to the barn in the middle of the night. It's a damn sight better than getting in my truck and drivin' five or ten miles."

"I'll bet." She couldn't wait to see if he'd followed her advice about the flower beds in his backyard. She'd make him carry her back there next.

Cal turned the final corner and stopped.

In front of her were two chicken coops, completely fenced in with chicken wire. "What's this?"

"This is yours."

She wiggled and said, "Put me down."

"Darlin', you don't have shoes on."

"So? Feet wash. I want a closer look."

He lowered her to the ground.

Kimi picked her way across the dirt. She curled her fingers through the holes in the chicken wire fence. Her heart raced like mad. These chicken coops didn't look brand new, but they didn't look used either. "You gonna tell me about these, cowboy? Or do I hafta guess?"

Cal moved in behind her, curling his hands around her hips and setting his chin on top of her head. "I started makin' these in my free time the fall after you left. The first hut was a piece of shit. I had my buddy's wife who raises chickens come and take a look at it. She told me to start over, and she lent me some coop plans. I finished these two styles and put them out here last summer. Built the fence around them this summer. As soon as you can find some chicks, you'll be in the chicken business. I know you need to make your own way, that don't have nothin' to do with *cow stuff*. I remembered you said you wanted to raise chickens, so here you go. This is all yours."

She tried to play it cool, like he hadn't just given her the best gift ever, but she was too emotional. She burst into tears.

He stiffened behind her.

She spun and wound her arms around his waist, pressing her cheek against his chest. When she gained a little control, she looked up at him.

"I hate seein' your tears, Kimi. I'm sorry—"

"Don't be. I'm just speechless. This is the best thing anyone has ever done for me in my entire life. Thank you." She cradled his face in her hands. "Thank you for understanding me, Cal. Thank you for waitin' for me. Thank you for loving me. Because god knows, I love you."

He closed his eyes. "Christ woman, you know how to get to the heart of a man."

"There's only one man's heart I want. Yours."

"You've got it." He opened his eyes and looked at her. "You've always had it. You always will." He kissed her with such tenderness, more tears flowed. "I love you," he murmured against her lips.

And then the reason for his insistence on her coming outside half-clothed became apparent. After a few more melting kisses, he whispered, "Ever done it against a chicken coop?"

She laughed. "No."

"Wanna give it a whirl?" He started planting kisses down her neck. "I can prove I'm cock of the walk."

She laughed again. "I don't have any chicken puns. But that'd be a hard one to top anyway."

"Is that a yes?" Cal smiled against her throat. "Or are you...chicken?"

"Hey, you cracked a...yolk."

He groaned. "That was terrible."

"I know. Maybe you'd better keep my mind and mouth occupied so I forget about the chicken jokes."

"My thoughts eggs-actly."

"Cal."

"Shut up and kiss me, woman. We'll see who comes first—and it ain't gonna be a chicken or an egg."

Cal convinced Kimi to go see Carolyn without him hovering, but he promised he'd show up at lunch time.

Kimi pulled up in front of the trailer and took a second to compose herself. There was a kids' plastic riding horse on springs on the small porch, as well as a couple of toy tractors. Even though it was early fall, pots of mums bloomed. And a few dozen canning jars were lined up on the bench.

It was stupid being nervous to see her sister.

So much had happened for both of them. They'd kept in touch, but even then they'd skirted their family issues.

Quick bein' a chicken.

Damn Cal and his chicken puns. But thinking of him allowed her to get out of the car.

Before she reached the bottom step of the porch, Carolyn was there, wrapping herself around Kimi and sobbing hysterically.

"You're really here! At first I thought maybe I dreamt it when Carson told me this morning that Cal had run into you last night at The Silver Spur. But when he reminded me again that you'd be coming by... I've been crazy to see you all morning." Carolyn squeezed her hard. "I missed you so much."

"I know. Me too."

"Why didn't you let me know you were coming?"

"I wanted it to be a surprise."

"Well, it's certainly that." Carolyn stepped back and wiped under her eyes. "Look at you. All lean and mean. I love the long hair. You look great, Kimi."

"Thanks." Kimi studied her sister. Carolyn had dark smudges from lack of sleep beneath her eyes, but two kids under four would contribute to that. Otherwise, she looked exactly the same as she had five years ago. Joyful. It was impossible to be around her and not let that same joy roll through her. "You haven't aged a day. You look happy."

"I am happy. Happier yet that you're here."

Kimi released a small gasp when she looked behind her sister and saw two little boys. Both dark-haired, both blue-eyed, both somber.

Carolyn turned and held her hand out to the youngest one. "Come and meet your Aunt Kimi, boys."

The older of the two launched himself off the porch, soaring past the two steps, his boots landing in the dirt with a soft thud.

His little cowboy hat was adorable. He tipped his head back and looked at Kimi. The kid was the spitting image of his father. She crouched in front of him. "Hi. I'm your Aunt Kimi."

He just blinked at her.

Carolyn tapped him on the shoulder. "Manners. Tell her your name."

"Cord West McKay."

Lord. He was just too damn cute for words. "Well, Cord West McKay, I'm happy to finally meet you."

Cord looked between Kimi and Carolyn and frowned.

"She's my little sister," Carolyn explained to him. "Like Colby is your little brother."

Kimi saw the younger boy propped on Carolyn's hip, his head resting on her shoulder. She pushed to her feet. "And who's this little doll?"

"Colby. Can you say hello to Aunt Kimi?" Carolyn prompted.

He buried his face in his mother's neck.

"He don't talk much," Cord informed Kimi.

"That just means I get to talk to you more."

"I got Lincoln logs," Cord said.

"I've never played with them. Maybe you could show me?"

Cord nodded. "Someday I'm gonna have a real log house."

"No!" Colby yelled. "Mine."

"No yelling at your brother, mister," Carolyn said. "You can share your toys."

"That always worked out so well for us," Kimi said dryly.

Then Colby held his arms out for Kimi to take him.

"That's new," Carolyn murmured when she handed him over. "He's in the *mama, mama, mama* stage."

"He's solid, isn't he?"

"Both of them take after their Daddy." She smoothed back Colby's dark hair. "Come inside. I put coffee on."

The inside of the trailer hadn't changed much, except now there were toys scattered around.

Colby wiggled to be let down and he and Cord scampered off down the hallway.

Carolyn poured two cups of coffee and gestured for Kimi to sit at the table. "I'd love for you to stay with me, but as you can see, there's not enough room here for us."

Kimi wrapped her hands around her cup. "I'm surprised with all the land the McKays are buying up that there hasn't been another ranch house you could move into."

"I stay out of ranch business. I'm sure as the wife of the oldest McKay there'll come a time when I'll have to be involved. But right now, taking care of my husband and two rambunctious boys, and doing piece work, keeps me too busy to worry about it."

She didn't respond; she just stared into her coffee cup.

An uncomfortable silence followed.

Carolyn sighed. "I'm sorry. I know we've avoided talking about this. Or maybe that's just me because I know I was wrong. I should've told you what was going on with Mom. I shouldn't have listened to Dad or Aunt Hulda." She fiddled with the crocheted coaster. "The fact I didn't know you'd had a big row with Mom and Dad that night after I got married... Honestly, I know now that what our dad and aunt wanted shouldn't have factored in at all, because neither of them could see past their animosity."

"How'd you find out about the fight?"

"Aunt Hulda told me when we discovered you'd taken off right after the funeral service." Carolyn's chin wobbled. "I felt like the most horrible person in the world, for not giving you the chance…" She held her hand over her mouth and started to cry.

Kimi stood and hugged her, letting her own frustrated tears fall.

When the crying had abated, Kimi said, "I was mad. I don't know if seein' her before she passed on would've made a difference, if I could've gotten over my anger at her, but I hated that I was the only one of all the kids who didn't get to make that choice."

"I know."

"And after I'd cooled off, I was still pissed on your behalf. I realized Dad would've expected you to do everything. Our brothers knew what was goin' on and they didn't help you, did they?"

For once, Carolyn didn't hedge and try to put a happy spin on it. She just shook her head.

"I'm sorry for that." She sighed. "I don't want this to have a hold over us anymore. So can we put it in the past?"

"It's already there, as far as I'm concerned." Carolyn dabbed at her eyes with a dishtowel. "I'm glad you're here, Kimi. And before I start grilling you about Cal, I need to know if I'm supposed to tell Dad or any of our brothers that you're back in Wyoming."

Kimi returned to her chair. "You're in contact with all of them?"

"Dad? Yes. He stops by to see the boys when he knows Carson isn't here. I want my kids to grow up around cousins since we didn't have that. I go over to Harland's because he's got a sweet little boy named Dag and Sonia doesn't seem to be in the best health. Darren has changed a lot since he and Tracy had their boy Luke. I hardly ever see Stuart and Janet. Thomas hasn't been home since Mom's funeral. Neither has Marshall after he took that job working for the railroad in Cheyenne."

"It's a happy thought, Caro, but with our brothers, if the apple doesn't fall far from the tree..."

"Wrong," she said with a sharp edge. "Kids are innocent. And just because someone was raised by shitty parents, that doesn't mean they'll automatically be shitty parents themselves. I'd never treat my boys the way we were treated."

Kimi set her hand over Carolyn's clenched fist, shocked that her sister had cursed. "I'm sorry. I didn't say that to piss you off. There's no doubt in my mind that you're a wonderful mother, and heaven knows you didn't have a great example."

"Thank you. Aunt Hulda said to me once that it's more important to be a good parent when you've had a lousy one just so you know it's a choice, not an inherited tendency."

"Smart woman, Aunt Hulda."

"Yes. So, enough about me. What's going on with you and Cal?"

This might prove tricky since she really didn't want to admit she'd been with Cal that week after the funeral. And if Carolyn had known about it, she would've brought it up. "We've stayed in touch over the years."

"Really? Why?"

"I like him. A lot. He's funny."

Carolyn's eyebrow rose. "Calvin McKay is funny? Like ha-ha funny?"

"Yep. And he's sweet, and thoughtful, and real." *And he is just as fantastic out of bed as he is in it.* "We've been pen pals and it just turned into something more."

"Did he know you were coming here?"

She nodded. "He just didn't know when."

That calculating look darkened Carolyn's eyes. "The chicken coops he built were for you?"

"Yeah."

"The fact he's gutted the entire second floor of his house and added a bathroom...that was for you too?"

"I don't know about that. To be honest, we didn't make it that far last night or this morning." As soon as she said that she blushed.

"So when you pulled into Wyoming, you went looking for him first?"

Crap. "Yes."

"And you two are more than friends?"

"Uh-huh."

"Then you're not here to visit. You're moving here. To be with Cal."

Kimi lifted her chin defiantly. "Yes, I am."

Carolyn shrieked and jumped up from the table. Then she pulled Kimi into her arms and danced around with her, laughing. "This is the best news I've ever heard! You're gonna be living up the road from me! Our kids will grow up together, and we can do things together all the time. Oh, Kimi, I'm so happy I could just scream!"

"Uh, you already did."

She laughed. "I've missed you so much. All the women around here are a lot older and they never want to talk about or do anything fun. All they do is complain."

"Well, the West girls are gonna shake things up for sure."

They grinned at each other goofily. Carolyn shrieked again and hugged her hard. "Love you, little sis."

"Love you too."

The door to the trailer opened. Two big men filled the doorway. Then two little boys came tearing down the hallway.

Carson scooped both boys up. "That's a fine welcome home at noon."

Kimi watched Cal watching Carson with his sons. Did Cal even realize he wore a look of longing? Then when his eyes met hers, it changed into a look of pure joy.

"Who wants ice cream?" Carson asked the boys. "Uncle Cal has said today is a day for celebrating and he's gonna buy us lunch in town."

"That sounds like a great idea. Why don't you get the boys in the car? I'll grab my purse and we'll be right out," Carolyn said.

Carson carried the boys out the door.

Cal started to follow but Carolyn grabbed him by the shirt sleeve. "Ah-ah-ah. Not so fast. I have something to say to you." She leaned in and got her mean face on. "Make my sister happy or else I'll gut you like a trout."

Kimi choked back a laugh.

"I've been waitin' for years for the chance to make her happy every day."

"Good. Then you *will* call the priest, or go to the justice of the peace, but I'll not stand for you two living together without being officially wedded. You hear me? No need for either of you to add to the McKays' bad reputation. So you've got a month to get it handled."

"Carolyn!"

Cal draped his arm around Kimi's shoulder and pulled her close. "No need to worry; I've got it covered."

Carolyn smiled and breezed out the door.

Kimi looked up at Cal and he kissed her before she got a word out.

When they broke free, she put her hand over his mouth so she could speak her piece. "I love my sister, but she doesn't get to set down ultimatums for us."

He nipped her fingers and she moved her hand. "Lord, woman, you think I don't know that? Do you really think a guy who built you two chicken coops doesn't have a plan?"

"Oh. Forget I said anything." She cocked her head. "Okay, so what's the plan?"

"I want to take you out on five dates." He kissed her. "One for every year you were gone."

"Cal. As of last night, we live together. Why do we need to date?"

"It'll make me happy. And I waited to be with you for five years; you can give me five dates before we make it official."

How did she ever get so lucky to be loved by this man? He'd loved her enough to let her go. And she'd loved him enough to come back. "Fine. But no fish places. If I never see a piece of Alaskan salmon or king crab again it'll be too soon."

Epilogue

Five months later...

Cal walked into the Dairy Queen and stopped in his tracks when he saw the hot-bodied blonde staring at him as she provocatively licked an ice cream cone.

Goddamn he loved her. Loved her like a crazy man. Things were better between them than he ever imagined they could be.

She sauntered closer. "Hey, handsome husband-to-be."

"Hey, beautiful bride-to-be. I thought I might find you here."

"I should hate that I'm so predictable." She licked her cone. "I delivered some eggs and I had a craving for ice cream." She looked at him. "Would you like some? I'm buying."

"Nope. I'm good." He put his hand on the small of her back and steered her to a booth along the wall.

After they sat, she eyed him warily. "What?"

"Darlin', we've gotta talk."

"About what? When I'm gonna make an honest man outta you?"

Cal had popped the question two weeks after she'd moved back to Wyoming, so they'd been engaged for four and a half months. But Kimi was dragging her feet on setting an actual wedding date. Part of that was because she'd been so busy getting her chickens all in a row with her egg business. The other part was she liked the notoriety of living in sin with a McKay. He wasn't pushing her; he had her in his bed every night and that's all that mattered to him.

Until now.

"No, darlin', we have to talk about your cravings."

"Are you worried I'm gonna let myself go and get fat now that I'm wearing your engagement ring?"

Jesus. "No. But sweetheart, you have been putting on some pounds—"

Splat. Kimi dropped her ice cream cone on the table and covered her hands with her face. Then she started crying.

Great. But he had no choice but to push her. "Kimi. Look at me."

"No! Why should I? Why would you even want to look at me? You think I'm fat!"

"No," he said calmly, "I think you're pregnant."

Her hands fell away. "What?"

"You're pregnant, aren't you?"

Surprisingly, she didn't hedge. "How'd you know?"

"Intuition."

"Because you work with pregnant cows all damn day?" she retorted.

Not touching that one. Avoiding the cone in the middle of the table, he picked up her hand and kissed her knuckles. "Have you talked to Caro about this?"

She shook her head.

"Why not?"

She bit her lip and stared at him.

"Are you upset that now it'll seem like we had a shotgun wedding?"

Again, Kimi shook her head.

"Darlin', you're scarin' me. What's goin' on?"

"Promise you won't get mad."

Fucking loaded question. "I promise."

"It's weird."

"I'm used to that with you."

"I've been planning to take you someplace fun for our honeymoon. I thought we could go to Florida or even California. I saved up a lot of money when I lived in Alaska, and I always wanted that to be travel money. But now, because I'm pregnant, we won't get to go. Probably we won't get to go anywhere besides Devil's Tower ever again."

Cal didn't understand the need to travel all over the damn place. But he knew people who loved it—his wife being one of those people. "I promise that we'll go other places besides Devil's Tower. We might not get to Paris or New York City while we're raising kids, but we can take a vacation someplace every year."

"I want that in writing because I know ranchers don't take sick days or vacations."

"Fine. We'll add it on as part of our wedding vows. Because, sweet darlin', you *are* gonna marry me as soon as possible. I'm thinkin' before the end of the week. And I promise you—our lives won't be over because we're havin' a baby."

"Okay."

He wasn't convinced she'd heard any of what he'd said. She'd been high and low in the last month—sometimes within mere minutes of one emotion overtaking the other, so her extreme reactions was more an indication of her pregnancy than the round middle she'd recently developed. "What else is on your mind?"

"That I'm a hypocrite."

He waited.

"I always swore I'd never be happy living in Wyoming. And yet, here I am, looking forward to spending the rest of my life right here with you."

"Sweetheart. That doesn't make you a hypocrite."

"What does that make me?"

"Smart enough to change your mind when you know you're part of a good thing."

She gave him a cocky smile. "Together we are a *great* thing." She glanced down at the ice cream cone melting all over the table. "Holy shit. Why didn't I notice this is making such a mess?" She slid out of the booth and raced to the counter, pulling napkins out of the dispenser, ran back to pick up the cone, then made a beeline for the garbage can, then back to the table.

He watched her with an amused expression. He'd nicknamed her the blonde tornado, but in her current emotional state he'd keep that to himself.

When she finally sat down, with another ice cream cone, she said, "What? Stop staring at me. I'm eatin' for two."

"That's not why I'm staring."

"Then why? You want a taste?"

"Of the ice cream? No. Of you? Like you wouldn't believe."

"And?" Kimi did a swirling thing with her tongue around the rim of the cone.

"And I'm havin' the same thought now as I had six years ago when I first saw you."

"What's that, cowboy?"

"That my cock is really jealous of that ice cream cone right about now."

She grinned. "Maybe I'm just practicing."

Cal pulled her out of the booth and scooped her into his arms. "I'm takin' you home so you can practice all you want."

She gave him a sticky-sweet kiss. "Drive fast."

WAIT! *You're not done! Turn the page to read Lorelei James' announcement about her new, exciting project that readers have been waiting for...*

Dear Reader,

When I ended the Rough Riders series in June 2014 with the last full length book, *Cowboy Take Me Away*, I promised my readers two things:

First, that I wouldn't leave the Rough Riders world entirely. When time permitted—and when inspiration struck—I'd write sneak peeks at the after the happily-ever-after like I did with the couples in *Short Rides*.

But as I started a story for Carter and Macie, and Colby and Channing for *Short Rides 2*, Cal McKay and Kimi West butted in and demanded I tell the origins of their love story first. So I did that with this novella, *Long Time Gone*. Never fear, I will write stories for the rest of the couples between working on other projects!

Second, I also promised my readers I wouldn't leave them hanging forever, waiting for Sierra Daniels McKay and Boone West, the young star-crossed lovers I introduced in *Gone Country*, Rough Riders book 14, published in December 2012, to get their story.

In my fictional world, Sierra and Boone, at ages sixteen and eighteen, needed time to grow up. In the real world, I needed time to figure out what to do with them. Since the main characters fall into both the McKay and West families, I could've put their story in either the Rough Riders world, or in the Wild West Boys world. Or I could start a whole new series. It was the "new" series that got me to thinking. Why not do a spin-off of the existing series?

Hence, the Rough Riders Legacy series has been born!

These third generation McKays and Wests are younger, for the most part, than their McKay parents were when they met, fell in love, and settled down. Since I've been forbidden from allowing anything to happen to the first generation (Carson and Carolyn, Cal and Kimi, Charlie and Vi, Joan) who were in their eighties at the end of *Cowboy Take Me Away*, this spin-off series will take place in the ten-year timespan between the last chapter and the epilogue of *Cowboy Take Me Away*.

What exactly does that mean? Since the characters in the Rough Riders Legacy series will be college-aged, their stories fall into the New Adult category of romance. Sierra, Kyler, and Hayden will be living away from the McKay stronghold in Wyoming. Not only will this allow them to learn to make their own ways; it also won't be necessary for new readers to be familiar with all 20+ installments in the original Rough Riders series to follow the stories.

I'm so excited to bring my readers something new, and yet something they've been asking for!

Lorelei

June 2015

Without further ado…

Read on for the exclusive excerpt of *Unbreak My Heart*,

the long-awaited story that reunites

Sierra Daniels McKay and Boone West.

I blame everything on the fever.

Everything.

My nausea.

My surliness.

My weepiness.

My utter lack of a reaction when he strolls into the exam room.

He gapes at me like I'm an apparition.

I continue to look at him blankly, as if it's no big deal he's here, right in front of me, wearing scrubs and a cloak of authority.

But the truth is I haven't seen him for six years.

Six. Years.

I should be in shock—maybe I'm in *too much* shock. This definitely falls under the heading of trauma. Because on the day he waltzes back into my life? I look worse than dog diarrhea.

I mentally kick myself for not going to the ER. Or perhaps just letting myself die. Anything would be better than this.

Screw you, universe. Fuck you, fate. Karma, you bitch, you owe me.

This chance meeting should've happened when I'm dressed to the nines, not when I sport yoga pants, a ratty Three Stooges

T-shirt, dollar store flip-flops and no bra. And the bonus? My hair is limp, my skin clammy, my face shiny from the raging fever I can't shake.

Wait. Maybe this *is* a fever-induced nightmare.

"Sierra?" The beautiful apparition speaks my name in a deep, sexy rasp.

Pretend you don't know him.

Not my most stellar plan, but I go with it.

I cock my head and frown as if I can't quite place him.

His expressive brown eyes turn hard. "That's really how you're gonna play this? Like you don't know me?"

I return his narrow-eyed stare because I'm too sick to fake an air of boredom.

"Fine. I'm Boone West. Your med tech," he says sarcastically. "I'm here to take your vitals."

I shake my head. My inability to respond isn't from pettiness—I lost my voice yesterday, due to this fever. But my middle finger works fine and I use it to point at the door as I mouth, "Get. Out."

"Nice try. But keep your arm out like that so I can take your blood pressure."

My heart rate skyrockets, so no freakin' way is he putting a blood pressure cuff and a stethoscope on me.

Boone moves in cautiously as if I'm a feral creature. He smiles—not the sweet, boyish grin I once loved—but one brimming with fake benevolence.

My belly flips, which pisses me off. And I wish projectile vomiting was my superpower instead of this uncanny ability to be at the wrong place at the wrong time, every time.

I jerk away from him.

"Look, Sierra," he says reasonably. "I wasn't expecting to run into you here. Not like this. Let me do my job and we'll talk afterward."

I shake my head so hard my vision goes wonky.

"It's not like you have a choice."

Wrong. In full panic mode, I bail off the exam table and hug the wall, facing him as I creep toward the door.

"Whoa. Slow down. You came into the clinic because you're sick. You can't just leave."

My throat feels like I gargled with gravel, but I manage, "Watch me."

Then I throw open the door and book it down the hallway.

But my fever has the last laugh.

My body chooses that moment to fail me. Chills erupt as if I've been plunged into a deep freezer, followed by sweat breaking out as if I've been baking in the Arizona desert. White spots obscure my vision.

I sway before everything goes dark.

"She's coming around."

I recognize that voice.

Dr. Monroe.

I peel my eyes open and notice I'm back in the exam room.

"Hey girl. How're you doin'?"

Girl. She seems to have forgotten that I'm not a girl, but a twenty-two-year-old college graduate with the world by the balls.

"I need to poke around, so lie still." She lifts my shirt and starts palpating my belly. For such a tiny thing, she pushes hard enough on my innards that I swear I feel her fingers poking the *inside* of my spine.

"Nothing out of the ordinary. Can you sit up?"

As soon as I'm upright, the whooshing sensation starts in my ears. My eyes burn but I can clearly see that Boone blocks the door. I grit out, "He goes."

Doc Monroe gets right in my face. "A patient who acts like they're trying to escape and then passes out in a waiting room full of people is hell on my reputation, Sierra McKay. Boone stays. You're lucky he acted so fast and caught you before you hit the floor."

"How did I...?" I gesture to the surrounding area.

"I carried you," Boone said. "You snuggled right into me. Strange behavior from someone who doesn't *know* me."

Goddammit. I hate this. I hate him. I level my best glare at his smarmy face.

He remains stoic.

Yeah, you were always good at hiding your emotions, weren't you?

"Sounds like you've got laryngitis too," Doc Monroe says. "Boone, you didn't get her vitals?"

"No, ma'am. Under the circumstances, maybe it's best if you do that."

The doc's gaze locks to mine.

"He has to go," I croak out.

"Sergeant West is here by government order, finishing the four week training stint in rural healthcare that the army requires for medical personnel at his level."

She didn't have to explain that to me. In fact, I really didn't want to know.

Doc sighs and takes my temperature, which tips the thermometer at a toasty 103 degrees. She checks my eyes, my ears and my nose. She presses her thumbs down the center of my neck and beneath my jaw. She listens to my lungs. Lastly, she shoves a tongue depressor in my mouth and shines a light in my throat while demanding I say *aaaaah*.

She pats my knee. "It appears you've got strep. But I'll send Sarah in from the lab for a throat culture to make sure."

No wonder I feel shitty and none of Rielle's natural home remedies worked on me.

Doc Monroe pokes the call button before she plops on the rolling stool and types on her laptop.

I stare at my knees, grateful I'm not wearing a drafty exam gown that leaves me even more exposed.

To Boone fucking West.

Two knocks sound on the door.

Boone steps aside as the lab tech hustles in.

"One quick swipe is all I need, no pokey pokes for blood tests," she chirps merrily.

I gag when she jams the long cotton swab into my throat and swirls it around.

"All done," she says with *way* too much fucking cheer.

She exits the room and Doc Monroe stands in front of me. "It'll be about fifteen minutes until I get the lab results. Why don't you lie down?"

I curl up on my side. Doc pulls out the exam table extension. Then she covers me with a blanket. Part of me wishes she acted cold and clinical instead of showing maternal concern.

The door shuts with a soft click.

Everything aches. My throat is almost swollen shut so it hurts twice as much to cry. But the tears leak out anyway.

"I'm still here," Boone states.

Go away.

"Since you can't talk, you'll damn well listen."

He's gotten bossier from his years in the military. But he struggles with whatever he wants to say since he remains quiet for longer than I expect.

"Of all the places in the country I could've chosen to complete this training assignment, I elected to do it here, in my hometown, because I wanted to see you again. Even when I suspected you'd kick me in the balls at best, or you were in a relationship with some undeserving douchebag at worst."

I hate that he tells me his worst case scenario is seeing me involved with someone else. Right then, I wish I had a hot, rich boyfriend with a big dick to flaunt at him.

"I don't know what surprised me more," Boone continues. "To find out that you actually changed your last name from Daniels to McKay—which is why with all the damn McKays around here I didn't know the *S McKay* on the patient chart was you—or that you no longer live in Sundance."

Even if my vocal chords weren't raw and nonfunctioning, I wouldn't respond. What can I say? He expects me to defend my choice to test my business skills beyond the Wyoming border? Screw that. He left for the very same reason. I owe him nothing.

"We're not done with this, Sierra. Not by a long shot."

His footsteps squeak on the linoleum. The door opens and closes with a soft click.

I know I'm alone.

Nausea rolls over me. I close my eyes.

I just need fifteen minutes and this nightmare will be over.

When Doc Monroe wakes me, I don't know where I am.

Then a cough and burning in my throat remind me.

"You tested positive for strep," the doc says, helping me sit up.

Goodie.

"Two treatment choices. A ten-day cycle of penicillin in pill form or a shot of penicillin."

"A shot," I whisper.

"Good choice. You'll feel better faster. You want me to prescribe a cough suppressant?"

I shake my head.

"Rielle's opinions of western medicine have rubbed off on you."

My father's wife prefers natural remedies whenever possible. Most people attribute that mindset to her hippie-like upbringing. But the truth is before she married my dad, her financial situation dictated she find fast and cheap alternatives. She and I laugh that she'd rather be seen as a hippie than a cheapskate.

The doc pulls out a syringe and a vial of clear liquid. She gets one affixed to the other and looks at me. "Drop your drawers. You get this shot in the butt."

Great. I hook my thumbs in my yoga pants.

Just then, three fast knocks sound on the door before it opens a crack. "Doc, we need you right away in six."

"Dammit." She gestures to me. "Get someone in here to do this."

That's when I know the universe is giving me an opportunity for payback, because fifteen seconds later, Boone strolls in, a needle in his gloved hand, looking nervous.

So the fever takes control. Or the bad angel. Or the devil in my soul that he put there when he left.

"I'm here to—"

"Give it to me, right?" I say huskily in my best phone sex operator voice. I turn around. Peering over my shoulder, I lock my gaze to his as I shimmy my yoga pants down to my knees.

He hisses in a breath. He's tempted to ditch decorum and drop his gaze from my face to my ass—which is completely bared by my thong.

My ass wins out.

Sucker.

And oops—I accidentally shake it at him as I lean over to rest my hands on the edge of the exam table.

"Hold still," he says tersely. He preps the area with a cool swipe of liquid on my skin.

I clench; I can't help it. Better that than him believing I break out in goose bumps from his simple touch.

"Relax," he murmurs.

Then before I fully prepare myself, he jams it in.

A soft grunt escapes me.

He soothes me, gently curling his hand around my hip. "Just a little more."

I know he's dragging this out. Big surprise that the bastard gets off on causing me pain. The injection site starts to sting, sending electric sparks shooting beneath my skin.

"Done."

Paper rattles and I look over my shoulder to watch him press a circular Band-Aid over the tiny dot of blood. Then he slowly sweeps his hand over my butt cheek.

I feel the pure male heat of him even through the latex.

"You can get dressed," he says without conviction or even looking at my face.

Asswipe.

I don't look at him as I yank my pants up.

Boone is still standing there when I turn around. "I'll come find you when you're feeling better so we can talk."

I shake my head.

"You can't escape the past, Sierra. More to the point, you can't escape me. See you around, McKay." Then he flashes that killer smile—my smile, the one he used to bestow only on me—and backs out of the room.

After that, I flee the office.

Two days later, I flee Sundance.

I tell myself I'm *not* fleeing from him.

I tell myself the only reason my dad let me know Boone stopped by a few hours after he saw me at the clinic was so I could avoid running into him again.

I'm in the clear now, with Wyoming in my rearview mirror and Arizona in my headlights.

But as the miles drag on, I can admit I did run from him.

I just didn't expect Boone West to chase after me.

Unbreak My Heart releases worldwide on February 8th, 2016 in all digital formats as well as print… Announcements for preorder links will be posted on *www.loreleijames.com* as soon as they're available.

Made in the USA
Middletown, DE
31 October 2015